To
Daneva
.

Blessing
Idaho author
Marilyn J. Harris

Song

Of the

River

- A Novel -

Marilynn J. Harris

Cottage Publishing

Cottage Publishing

Boise, Idaho

www.marilynnjharris.com

First published by Cottage Publishing 5-16-2017

ISBN-13: 978-1546980162 (CreateSpace)

ISBN-10: 1546980164

Printed in the United States of America

For information or to order more books please visit our website:

www.marilynnjharris.com

Or Contact:

Cottage Publishing

8530 W Targee Street

Boise, ID 83709

To our Sunday after church

Lunch Bunch

Table of Contents

One

Talking with Uncle Harry

As I was growing up, my favorite person in all of the world was my Uncle Harry. He was kind, intelligent, and knowledgeable about everything. One day as we were talking he asked me, "Harrison, have you ever been someplace, maybe in a new city, where you know that you have never been before? Yet as you look around you realize everything looks hauntingly familiar. The streets, the old buildings, the run-down houses. The closer you get to the center of the town, the eerier everything seems." He continued, "Your skin becomes clammy, and the hair on the back of your neck stands up straight."

He told me, "Suddenly, you feel nauseated and the air is so heavy you can barely breathe. Your entire body goes rigid, and you cannot move your legs. You fear your heart will burst, because it is beating so rapidly." He shook his head back and forth very slowly as he continued, "With each step, you try to convince your mind that everything will be alright. You pretend

1

to be calm, as if you have nothing to fear. Yet, as you walk towards the old building in front of you, the dread grows stronger and stronger, and you know that somehow you have been there before. Your logic tells you that it couldn't be, yet your mind sees what lies beyond every door."

He hesitated before going on, "As you move up to the front entrance of the building, your brain can readily describe the inside of the main doorway, even before going in. You know exactly what the massive conference room looks like that is hidden behind the thick wooden doors."

Uncle Harry smiled before going on, "Suddenly you notice a large familiar image off in the distance. A giant statue. The white porcelain statue is sitting on a massive carved table over against the back wall. You recognize the unique statue, and know that you have seen it numerous times before, but you have no idea where."

He continues, "As you head towards the conference room, your memory once again recalls every detail of the room behind the doors. It is a very large room decorated with bold flowered carpeting, antique velvet chairs, and a giant oak desk sitting proudly between two vast windows. As you enter the room, you can instantly tell that nothing in the room has been changed since the building was first constructed many years earlier."

My uncle pauses before saying, "You recall the stale musty smell of cigar smoke as it permeates throughout the entire room after years of being used as a smoking chamber for mayors, judges and other prominent figures. You feel confused, because you can't remember being in this place before, but your intelligence reminds you that somehow you recall ever detail of the area." This was Uncle Harry's world. His ambiguous life was filled with unanswered questions, and new beginnings.

My uncle was born Harrison Obadiah Pike, but everyone in our family just called him Uncle Harry. I am proud to say that my name is also Harrison; Harrison Lee Hayes. I was named Harrison after my illustrious Uncle Harry.

When I was a young child, I would sit for hours and listen to him talk. He was so interesting and he had so many stories to tell. Sometimes I questioned how one person could have lived such an unusual life. However, my parents assured me that all of the stories he told me were true, and I was mesmerize by the places he talked about.

Even though I was a child and he was old enough to be my grandpa, I was completely absorbed when he spoke. He had been through so much in his lifetime and he had such a wealth of information to share. He talked to me as if I were older and we were on the same level. He rarely treated me like a child, he treated me more like a friend. I often forgot about our age difference. Besides, when you are young it is difficult to guess the age of an older person, because every grown-up seems old to you. Uncle Harry was active and spry, but I knew from the things that he talked about that he had been living for a lot of years.

My dad and mom owned a grocery store and they worked all of the time, so I never spent the time talking to my dad like I did my Uncle Harry. My dad was always busy. It was just Uncle Harry and me and my sister until my parents got home in the evening.

My sister Caryn and I liked having someone there waiting for us when we got home from school every day. We felt safer just knowing that there was an adult in the house when we came home.

I loved to hear my uncle's stories, Uncle Harry told me of things that most people only read about in history books. He was probably the most accomplished person that I have ever met in my life, and he was an excellent story teller.

My uncle had such a mystifying upbringing, and that seemed to make his facts even more interesting to me. He was extremely intelligent and he would continually remind me that every person has a story to tell; and no one will ever know your story unless you pass it on.

Marilynn J. Harris

Uncle Harry had an old picture album that he left out on the table next to his bed. I often sat for hours and looked through the old album. He did not have any baby pictures of himself or his family, but the pictures of him as a young boy were very striking. He grew up to be over 6 feet tall, with thick dark perfectly combed hair and blazing dark blue eyes.

In every picture, he appeared to stand up straight and proud showing off his impeccable white teeth and his boyish confident smile. He was always the charming gentleman. I am sure he melted quite a few ladies' hearts in his younger days.

When he wasn't paying attention to me, I would study the picture album and then look at him from across the room. He hadn't really changed all that much. He was still tall and slender, and rather distinguished looking. Only his thick dark hair had changed, it was now a glistening bright white color with slivers of silver streaming through it. He was so polite and dignified, and he was kind to everyone. I thought he was absolutely amazing, so he appeared the same to me, as he did in the old pictures.

He had seen so much of the world; both good and bad, and my Uncle Harry was a survivor. I thought he was the smartest and most wonderful person ever born. I wanted to be just like him someday. Although Uncle Harry had been a widower all of my life, the old album showed pictures of a beautiful young wife and two small children. So, I knew that he had once been married and had at least two children during his lifetime, but for some reason they were all gone by the time I was born.

One of my favorite pictures was of Uncle Harry standing next to a stunning gold Palomino horse with a light-colored main and tail. It was one of his earliest photos. Uncle Harry was about five years old in the picture, and he was leaning up against the horse with one arm draped around the horse's neck. I could tell that he really loved that horse by the way he comfortably hung over it, and he was beaming from ear to ear as he hugged the side of its head.

Even as an older gentleman, he was still gracious and well-liked. He was witty, intelligent and easy to talk to, so he had several lady friends at church that he often met for lunch or dinner. Many of the widows brought him homemade jam, fresh rolls, scones or warm applesauce cake with cream cheese frosting. Some brought him freshly baked sugar cookies, berry cobbler or his favorite, lemon meringue pie. Uncle Harry was always generous to share his freshly-baked goodies with my sister and me. We loved to see his lady friends come calling.

Our family home was very large and Uncle Harry had rented one of the upstairs rooms. Ever since I could remember, he had always been there, he was just part of our family. Each day he was there waiting for us when we got home from school. My sister was two years older than me, so after we finished our afterschool snack she would go upstairs and read, and I would sit and visit with my Uncle Harry. We'd play our daily game of chess, and then talk and laugh for hours.

I look back now, and I realize that it was because he was older that he had the time to talk with me. My parents were always busy working at their store, so they seemed thankful that Uncle Harry was there and we were never left alone all afternoon.

My grandmother lived with us too, and sometimes it was my grandma that would be waiting for us, but usually it was Uncle Harry. He never seemed to mind, and he took his job very seriously. He made sure we got home safely each day. If we were late getting home after school, he would come looking for us.

My uncle and I could talk about anything. I would chatter away about my day at school, and he always seemed genuinely interested. We both loved basketball, trains, history and chess so we never ran out of things to talk about. Each day when we came home from school Uncle Harry would be waiting for us at the front door, smiling and eager to greet us. He seemed as excited to see us, as we were to see him.

Marilynn J. Harris

Uncle Harry was the one person in my life that really listened to me. I was lucky because most of my friends didn't have someone like Harry to talk too. He made me feel like I was an important person, he had a way of making me feel like whatever happened in life would be ok. I always felt uplifted when I talked things over with him. My sister Caryn told me years later that she was often jealous of the closeness that I had with our uncle.

****

One afternoon when I came running down the street after school, I noticed that Uncle Harry was not standing at the door waiting for us, as he always did. I instantly felt panicked. The closer I got to the house the more worried I became. I saw my parent's car parked out in front of the house, and I knew something was wrong.

As I burst in the front door hollering for Uncle Harry, I became even more frightened, because I couldn't find him anywhere. I ran from room to room shouting his name, but he never answered me. I wanted to tell him that I had won the spelling Bee at school.

Suddenly, my mother walked out of the kitchen drying her wet hands on a dish towel after she heard me shouting throughout the house. Tenderly touching my hands she bent down and quietly told me, "Now Harrison stop shouting for Uncle Harry, he is just upstairs." She got an odd look on her face as she looked toward the stairs before going on, "I'm sorry Harrison, but Uncle Harry is upstairs packing because he is getting ready to leave." She knew that I was going to be upset about him leaving so she talked even softer trying to break the news to me gently.

She said, "Uncle Harry needs to go back to Oklahoma for a while, he needs to be closer to his sister. He just got word this morning that she isn't well and she needs him to come home right away." My mom sadly shook her head back and forth and said, "Uncle Harry is the only sibling that she has left, and she has been asking for him, so he will be leaving immediately."

I stared up at my mother in shock, "Will he be gone long?" I asked, already fearing the answer.

"Now Harrison, I'm not sure how long he will be gone. But he is leaving on the 4:30 train," she told me as she walked back into the kitchen letting me know that the conversation was over.

I was devastated. Uncle Harry had always been there for me. He had moved in when I was just an infant, and it never entered my mind that he would one day leave. I couldn't believe that he would no longer be waiting for me when I came home from school. We were his family. I was barely ten years old and I just didn't understand why he was leaving. I was devastated. I felt like I was losing one of my parents.

I watched out my bedroom window as my father piled my uncle's luggage in the backseat of our old Hudson. Then I slowly walked downstairs to say goodbye. After I hugged Uncle Harry that one last time, I ran to my room and cried and cried and I wouldn't come out. I feared I would never see him again, and I don't think Uncle Harry realized how much he meant to me. I was just a child, so he probably was much more important to me than I was to him.

That night at dinner, my mom tried to make me feel better about Uncle Harry's leaving and she told me, "I think the reason that you and Uncle Harry got along so well was because you both have the same name and you are so much alike."

My mom was right, we understood each other, but it was much deeper than that. I was just a young person, yet he always took the time to talk to me, and he really listened when I talked. Uncle Harry was a strong believer in God, so he told me bible stories, he taught me memory verses, and he never let me forget how much God loved me. He made me feel important. No one could understand, but he was my best friend.

The next day when I got home from school, I sadly walked into Uncle Harry's room and closed the door and cried my eyes out. His room looked almost the same. He left everything in place, as if he truly planned to return, but I knew in my heart that I would never see him again.

I dried the tears from my eyes and walked back into my bedroom. The first thing that I saw was the train set that Uncle Harry had given me for Christmas, only a few months earlier. I had loved that train more than any other gift in this world, and I played with it every single day. My dad, and Uncle Harry and I had set up the complete village in my room. It had small buildings, bridges, and several feet of extra track. Now, with Uncle Harry gone, it saddened me to even look at it.

After Uncle Harry left, he often wrote to my mother but he only wrote to me one time. At first I thought about him every single day, and I silently cried alone in my room. I missed him so much. I had so many things to tell him about, and I still had countless unanswered questions that I needed to ask him. For weeks after he left I fretted about him being gone, and I mourned his leaving.

Every night I prayed that the Lord would allow me to meet with him, just one more time. One more time to tell him thank you, to let him know how important he was to me; but that one more time never came. I've thought about him hundreds of times throughout my lifetime, and the impact he had on my life. Sometimes we only need one other person in our life to believe in us, and to make us feel good about ourselves. I was lucky that I had that one person encouraging me in the early years of my life.

It took me months after he left, to accept the fact that he was never really coming back. I hated to give up hope. It was like he died that very day; the day he drove away with my dad to catch the train.

I never played with my train set again after he left. Within a few months my mother boxed up it up, and stored it away, and I never saw it again. A short time later she also removed the chess set that the two of us had always played. My mom said it just cluttered the room, and besides I no longer had anyone to play chess with.

As I grew older, I played basketball for my school, and there wasn't one game that I ever played in that I didn't think of Uncle Harry. I wished he could have been there to cheer me on. He loved basketball, and I had become a pretty good basketball player. I know that if he could have he would have been in the front row hollering the loudest.

One of the greatest lessons that I learned from my Uncle Harry was how much wisdom older people have to share, if only the younger generation will listen. He helped me to be a better student in school, and he taught me to always do my very best at everything that I did. My uncle initiated a desire in me to learn more about God's creation, the history of the world, and especially about the places that he talked about in his stories.

He taught me to accept other people, to never be prejudiced, and to always respect my elders. Because of his strong belief in God, my faith continued to grow throughout my lifetime. I married a Christian girl, and we raised three Christian believers, who gave us seven Christian grandchildren.

Uncle Harry was by far the greatest inspiration in my life. He made such a lasting impression on me that I grew up and became an American History Professor. After I got married, my wife and I took several trips searching for the places that he had told me stories about. We have been all over the United States, and we have tried to visit every old town or community that I could remember him speaking of. Some of the places we visited, we traveled by train, just like Uncle Harry did.

My wife was a High School Social Studies teacher with classes in geography, civics, history and economics. While following the paths of Uncle Harry she enjoyed visiting various places that she had taught about in her classes. I was fortunate to have a wife that was willing to just take off and go with me in search of Uncle Harry's past. She knew how important he had been in my life.

Marilynn J. Harris

Many of the places and events that my uncle talked about happened over 100 years ago. They are now empty wastelands or deserted ghost towns, but it was interesting just to go and walk the land and experience so much of the history that he had told me about.

Years Later After I Retired

Marilynn J. Harris

Two

Cleaning out the Attic

After I retired from teaching at the college, I went home to Memphis for a few weeks to help my parents clean out their garage and attic so that they could sell their property. My folks had lived in their house for over 60 years and their entire place was full of antiques, old furniture and boxes that they had inherited throughout the years from deceased family members.

My mom and dad had a large rambling country home with lush green lawns, assorted flowerbeds, stone walkways and many fruit trees. It was the same notable house that I had been raised in, but the property had been sold recently to be used as a bed and breakfast. The house is large with many bedrooms, and the grounds are fastidious, so it will be a perfect site for the new owners that will be moving in within the month.

Although my parents still loved their beautiful home they were getting older and it was becoming too much for them to take care of. They were ready to downsize and find an easier way of life in a private gated community.

None of our family members lived close enough to help with the yardwork or the upkeep on the household residence. Everyone had moved away from the area. I had moved my family clear across the United States to Boise, Idaho, over thirty years ago. I taught at Boise State University, and Boise is over 1900 miles away from my parent's house in Memphis.

The homestead property was good-sized and my parents had been hiring much of the yardwork done for the past several years. My sister and her family lived at least 10 hours the other direction, so there was no one close-by to help our parents. Even though it was emotional for all of us, the time was right for them to sell it and move away.

My parents had outlived most of their family members and as a result they had acquired many lavish possessions from their departed relatives. Everything in the garage and attic was stacked and organized, but they had so many things that there was no way for them to sort through everything on their own.

My mom and I started with the garage and after two long days, we had it all sorted out and cleaned. She helped me a lot, but she was worn-out and it was time for me to tackle the attic alone. My dad had cut his hand while he was packing his tools in his workshop the day before I arrived, so he was unable to help at all. His cut was deep; he had fourteen stiches in his hand, and because he had lost so much blood the doctor insisted that he rest and keep his hand elevated.

Both of my parents were in their mid-eighties, and I knew that they could not do all of this moving on their own. It was just too much for them to go through everything by themselves. There was a lot to sort through, because they had lived in this house for so many years, and they had accumulated things their entire married life. Even with everything neatly packed in boxes it was overpowering.

After breakfast one morning, I climbed the steep stairs to the loft, and started sorting out the attic by myself. The attic too was overflowing with family treasures. There were boxes and furniture stacked, floor to ceiling, from one end of the large room to the other. I diligently worked for several hours before stopping for a sandwich, coffee and a short restroom break, then it was back to sorting again.

I continuously worked until late in the evening trying to sort out all of the boxes and valuables piled throughout the large upper room. It was difficult for me to tell what was important and what to discard. I knew that whatever I chose to keep, my mom and dad would have to decide who to give it to. They had already been asking all of the grandkids, nieces, nephews and close friends to choose what they would like. Everyone said they had collected enough junk of their own over the past few years, and they didn't need any more clutter to add to their own encumbered mess, so I was a bit overwhelmed with so many decisions.

I felt weary from all of the sorting and from moving so many heavy objects. I couldn't tell a valuable antique clock from a box of cut-up material that some aunt had saved to make a quilt. My eyes were blurry and my mind was on over-load, but I knew that I was the only person that could clean out the attic. My parents were too old to climb up and down the steep stairs anymore, and my sister Caryn, was recuperating from back surgery.

By the fourth day, I was exhausted, I had sorted through over half of the sealed boxes. I had carried many lamps, pictures, small tables, dishes, and a variety of glass bottles down the stairway for my parents to look through. My goal was to completely empty out the attic by the end of the week, but my brain was dealing with a mixture of emotions as I worked. The sorting was very emotional for me, because this was the house that my sister and I had been raised in, and I was cleaning it up and preparing it for someone else to own. It will no longer be a place for us to come home to for holidays and birthdays. This home has always been a welcoming refuge for all of the grandchildren and great-grandchildren to gather and share as a family.

The magnificent treehouse that my dad and I built for all of the grandkids, and great-grandchildren, must be left behind in the huge old oak tree. The tall sturdy rope swing with its recently replaced sections will no longer be used by anyone in our family during summer picnics or after backyard baseball games. We will never again hear the laughter and giggles of our younger generation as they take their turn running and playing throughout the meticulous backyard. My heart can't help but be filled with overpowering sadness, because this will be the end of an era for our entire family.

My mind was completely jumbled after days of digging through box after box of my deceased relative's priceless possessions. Belongings that I knew nothing about. Items that at one time were cherished and held at only the highest esteem by someone. Objects that now were sealed tightly inside a cardboard box for a stranger like me to sort through and decide what is important and what is to be discarded. Each box held a lifetime of someone's memories, and I felt very frustrated.

It was time for me to stop for a few hours and get a cup of coffee and something to eat. All of the sorting was taking a toll on me, my back was aching and my eyes were starting to burn. I was beyond discouraged. I really wanted to just be done with everything.

The thought crossed my mind to throw my hands in the air and walk away and give anything that was left in the attic to some charity. I didn't feel like looking through any more old treasures. There was just too much stuff; I could see no end in sight. As I ranted and raved, I made a silent promise to myself that I would never leave rubbish and old containers full of worthless nothingness like this for my three children to sort through.

I planned to clean out my own cluttered attic as soon as I returned to Idaho. I knew that I had old junk stored up there that I have not even looked at for over twenty years. I have things that no one will ever care about or even keep. It was time to go through it and get rid of things so that my family won't have to sort and clean everything up after my wife and I are gone. Sorting through all of someone else's worldly possessions is a very emotional, back-breaking endeavor, and I would not wish this job on anyone.

I stood up to stretch and I was about to leave the attic when a large box over in the corner of the room caught my eye. Boldly written across the top corner of the box in big black letters it said, **Harrison Andrew Obadiah Pike-Langley.** The box had been mailed from Oklahoma. The package was registered, and it had been signed for. As I looked closer I realized the package was addressed to me, Harrison Lee Hayes, at our home address here in Memphis.

The cardboard box had been hidden on the bottom of the pile, underneath several other boxes that I had been going through in the past few days. I had finally moved enough of the top boxes that I could easily see the container that had been buried out of sight until now.

I felt numb as I recalled the many childhood memories of my favorite Uncle Harry, and for one second it seemed like it was just yesterday. I couldn't help myself, the exhaustion had suddenly disappeared, and I was filled with a new energy. I sat down right there in the center of all of the clutter and began to tear open the memorable box. My legs felt weak and I was quivering all over, I couldn't believe it, I had just uncovered a message from my long-lost friend.

My hands would not stop shaking as I cut the discolored tape that had held the antique box together for so many generations. As I tore open the old cardboard box I could tell that it had never been looked through or even touched. Carefully cutting down the sides of the sealed box I discovered a black metal chest placed skillfully inside the walls of the cardboard container. I reverently cut the box away until only the metal chest could be seen.

I just sat and stared at the perfectly preserved black chest. It was so like Uncle Harry to organize his life story and keep it meticulously placed in a fire-proof container for me to discover years after it had been sent.

When I opened the container, I couldn't believe my eyes. There were hundreds of pages of hand-written notes and the old papers were in pristine condition. They had been carefully preserved inside the metal chest, and packed inside the cardboard box for over fifty years.

Promptly I glanced around the room to find a more comfortable place to sit. I noticed an old rocking chair over in the corner, by the window, and I began to drag the bulky metal container across the attic floor. The chest was quite heavy, but I could hardly wait to begin my examination of my glorious find. My Uncle Harry had been my inspiration, my motivation and my closest childhood friend.

As I sat quietly holding the cherished binders for several seconds, my pent-up emotions could not be contained. The past few days had been an ominous roller coaster of sentiments and sadness. I could no longer hold back the humble tears of emotion that were easily gliding down my face. After all of these years, my beloved uncle had finally returned; one more time, just as I had prayed.

I looked at my watch it was 2:05 P.M. and I hadn't had a break since breakfast. As anxious as I was to get started, I decided to stop for a few minutes then get a fresh start reading when I got back. It was time for a sandwich and some hot coffee.

When I went downstairs, I first went to the bathroom, and as I walked into the kitchen I calmly asked my mother, "Do you remember getting a package from Uncle Harry many years ago? I found a large box with his name on it, up in the attic."

My mother got a strange look on her face and said, "Oh Harrison, I'm sorry I never even opened it. He sent it to you special delivery, years ago. I signed for it the day it came, but I never took the time to look inside." She shrugged her shoulders and then sadly put her head down before saying, "Your grandmother had passed away, World War II had ended, and of course we had the store to run, and you had just entered Junior High school. There was a lot going on at that time. Besides you had finally adjusted to Uncle Harry being gone, so I never mentioned the package to you. We never even knew when he passed away."

She muttered on, "I was really busy, so I just signed for it, and had the delivery man carry the heavy package up to the attic, and I stored it away. I forgot it was even up there."

I hadn't ever noticed until then, but my mother seemed almost jealous of the close relationship that I had with Uncle Harry. I wanted to say to her, "You forgot it for over fifty years?" But I could tell that she was already embarrassed by all of the stacks of boxes that I had been going through for her, so I kept quiet.

I'm sure that she was wishing that she had taken the time to sort through everything herself years ago, when she was still able to. I was named after my uncle, but I had to remember that Uncle Harry was probably never as important to my mother, as he was to me.

I just smiled and hugged her shoulders, and went over and sat down. I cheerfully ate the ham sandwich, chips and macaroni salad that she had prepared for me. I drank a full glass of cold water, and told her, "Thanks for the lunch." Before heading back to the attic I reached across the table and grabbed three warm freshly-baked chocolate chip cookies to go with my cup of hot coffee. It was time to head back upstairs and get started on my reading.

I got comfortable in the corner chair before picking up the first few pages of the manuscript. Everything seemed unreal, yet I was so elated to find the manuscript that I felt like I was getting ready to watch one of my favorite old movies. I just held the first few pages in my hands for several seconds trying to grasp the magnitude of what I had discovered. I took a

Marilynn J. Harris

deep breath and leaned back and began my reading. I could hardly wait; the story began in 1867 the year Uncle Harry was born.

1867
The Life Story
Of
Uncle Harry

Marilynn J. Harris

Three

Harrison Andrew Obadiah Pike-Langley

By Harry Pike-Langley

I, Harrison Obadiah Pike, was born on April 16, 1867 somewhere in a small town in the United States of America. I was told that at the time of my birth my family lived in a rundown four-room shack with dirt floors, boarded up windows and straw filled bags that had been sewn together and placed around on the floor to be used as beds for everyone to sleep on.

I was the ninth child born to Ben and Isabella Pike. I was told that I arrived in the middle of the night, in a dark corner of the main living quarters of the house. Like so many babies born at that time, I was delivered by my grandmother. When I came into this world, there was no fanfare or excitement about my birth. Only my grandmother, my father, and of course my mother were aware of my arrival. All of the other family members were soundly sleeping around us throughout the room. I was very tiny because I was a twin, and we had been born two weeks early. My twin brother Henry

23

died at birth, leaving me alone to survive the world on my own. I guess my mother almost bled to death during our delivery and after I was born, she went into shock and couldn't move or talk.

After we were delivered, they placed my dead twin brother in a small box and took him outside to be buried, then my grandmother wrapped me tightly in a corn sack cloth and placed me near the wood burning stove to keep me warm until they could decide what to do with me. She knew that I would die too if she did not find a wet nurse to care for me. My mother was only semi-conscious and she was unable to even hold me. My grandmother was forced to make a rapid decision to get me taken care of so that she could concentrate all of her energy on my mother and my brothers and sisters.

My brother and I were the ninth pregnancy for my parents in fourteen years, and my mother was only 29 years old. She had been having children since she was fifteen, and I guess this pregnancy was just too hard on her body. After she delivered me, she was bleeding so profusely that my father and my grandmother knew that she would not live through the night. It was such a horrendous time for both of them, that all they could think about was getting me away.

My grandmother knew of a black woman and her family that had moved to this area a few years ago. The family had been set free by the emancipation proclamation issued by President Abraham Lincoln on January 1, 1863, only a few years earlier. The woman had recently been serving as a wet nurse for several rich white families, and she lived only a few hours away. Everyone called the woman Aunt Etta. Aunt Etta had saved many newborn babies who had lost their mothers during childbirth.

A wet nurse is a woman who breast feeds and cares for babies that are not her own children. She takes care of other women's babies when they are unable to feed and care for the babies themselves. Many wet nurses could feed up to five different babies at one time. This was a very valuable service before baby formulas were invented. If there were no wet nurses available most of the babies in need would just starve to death.

I was told that my father woke up my older sister and sent her to retrieve the neighbors and their wagon to take me to the wet nurse. My father and my grandmother felt that they didn't dare leave my dying mother so they asked the neighbors if they could take me on my journey. Apparently my parents and the neighbors were very close friends and they were continually there to help each other in any time of need.

The man worked with my father, and his wife was like a sister to my mother. They lived only a few houses away in a run-down house much like ours. Most of the people in the area didn't have a lot. Asking these people to take me on this trip, in the middle of the night, was a huge request for my dad and grandmother to ask of them, but I was later told that they helped out without even hesitating.

When they arrived with the wagon, my grandmother rapidly gave me the name Harrison Obadiah Pike, the name my mother had planned to name me. She wrote my name and my date of birth down on a piece of plain white paper. She folded up the piece of paper and handed it to the neighbor lady to be given to Aunt Etta and her family so that they would know my name. Within minutes, my grandmother had me wrapped tightly in an old blanket and she kissed my cheek and placed me in the arms of the neighbor lady, and I was gone.

Four

Aunt Etta

So much of my story had to be told to me when I was older because I was just an innocent newborn with no recollection of my own. I was told that I stubbornly screamed and wailed the entire trip in the jostling old wagon. Yet the faithful neighbors continued the difficult journey for the rest of the night, trying desperately to get me to this savior woman, known only as Aunt Etta.

I was tiny and cold, and I was later told that they continually prayed that I would stay alive long enough to get me to the wet nurse where I could be taken care of. Even through my screaming, they moved forward through ruts, mud holes, and freezing rain.

At daybreak, we arrived at the modest shack of Etta and Titus Lewis and their seven children. Aunt Etta came running to meet us at the front door once she heard me screaming outside. She instantly took my tiny body from the stranger's arms to try to keep me quiet, so that I would not wake up the rest of her family.

Aunt Etta knew nothing of my coming, but she could tell by my screeching that I was a child in need. She went straight to work giving me the milk of life, and I instantly became spine-chillingly quiet.

The lady who had brought me in the wagon had tears streaming down her face as she handed the white piece of paper to Aunt Etta. She also gave her a small bag of coins that my grandmother had sent for her. She rapidly told her, "The child's name is Harrison Obadiah Pike," and then she quickly ran back out the door and returned to the wagon and rode away with her husband.

"Harrison Obadiah Pike, Harrison Obadiah Pike, Harrison Obadiah Pike," Aunt Etta repeated over and over again so to keep the name to memory. Looking down at the fragile infant that she had been handed, Aunt Etta grinned and said, "Well little Harrison Obadiah Pike, I am glad the lady told me your name because neither I nor my husband Titus can read this piece of paper." Still staring down at the now peacefully sleeping newborn she whispered, "We might have been forced to call you Screech cause of the awful screeching sounds I first heard." Aunt Etta had a magic touch because even as she talked, I remained sound asleep.

For the next several weeks, I continued to flourish. I grew bigger and stronger because I was given such wonderful care. Aunt Etta's entire family helped take care of me, even her seven children, and her husband Titus helped, and I became healthier every day.

Each day Etta and Titus Lewis waited for word from my family, but no word ever came. Of all of the babies that Aunt Etta had helped, she had never had this happen before. She usually just kept the infants during the critical stage of their life, until they were strong enough to go home to their families.

Most of the relatives visited their infants every day when she fed them. Aunt Etta had not been feeding many babies recently. In fact, I was the only infant that she was caring for at that time. She had expected to hear word from my family after the first few days, because someone had already given her coins in advance for her help. Still, no one had ever returned to get me, so she had no idea where I had even come from.

Titus worked as a janitor at the court house and his job was to clean the building every evening after everyone had gone home. He often took me with him when he went to work, just to give Aunt Etta a break for a while. He would put me on a blanket over in one corner of the room, and then he would go about doing his work. He took me to work with him even after I got older, but we never saw any other people and Titus worked alone.

Several months passed and there had still been no word as to who I belonged to. No one came to check on me, or to even see if I had survived. All Aunt Etta and Titus knew was that I was a chubby little white child by the name of Harrison Obadiah Pike. The people of the black community were the only people that I ever saw. The black community kept to themselves, and I never saw any outsiders. As I continued to grow, I never saw another white person.

Months went by and gradually the months turned into years and after being with Aunt Etta and Titus for so long they no longer looked for anyone to come and get me. I was just accepted as another member of the family; they had no choice. It had been almost three years, and I was treated just like everyone else in our black community. I didn't even know that I was different, because I had never seen anyone outside of our group. Living with Aunt Etta and Titus and their children was all that I knew.

Many of the families in our small community had grown unhappy living in this region, and they talked of going back to the south. They had lived together in this area since they had gained their freedom, but they were often sad and lonely. Their lives were not easy. They were set apart from everyone else in the town, and things had not worked out the way they had hoped that they would. When they were first freed from slavery, they tried to get as far away from the South as possible, but they had been away for several winters and they now felt it was time to go back home. Many white families as well as black families were beginning to migrate further south at that time.

The people that had jobs, gave notice that they were moving, and early one spring morning each family collected everything that they owned, and we started the challenging journey south where many of their relatives still remained. They had heard reports that things were getting better for the black people in the South all of the time. Many of the people were getting educated and finding good jobs, and they had received word that the organized group called the Ku Klux Klan had been almost completely terminated. They felt sure that it was now safer for them to move back home where they had come from.

I was fair-skinned with blonde hair and dark blue eyes, but Aunt Etta and Titus and the children treated me like I belonged to them. Of course if anyone ever saw me they would know that I didn't, but I was healthy and safe and always fed, and these people were the only family that I knew. They had no choice but to take me with them when they moved. I had been with them for three years, and even if I didn't really belong to them, I didn't really belong anywhere else either.

Aunt Etta, Titus and their children had taught me to walk and talk and to love everybody. I thought I was just one of their children and I would live with them forever. I felt like Nicolas, Mary, Ronald, Carolyn, Constance, Richard and MeriEllen were all my brothers and sisters.

Nicolas was the oldest, he was tall and strong, and he always played games with me and he let me follow him around. When I got old enough, he was the one who taught me how to walk. He was very patient and he never got upset with me. He just encouraged me until I would let go of his fingers, and start walking. I loved being around Nicolas, he was a good big brother.

Marilynn J. Harris

Mary was quiet, gentle and kind to me. She continually carried me with her everywhere she went until I was about two years old. That was fine with me, because I loved being carried, and I loved being the baby of the family.

Ronald like to build things. He would often play alone at the far end of the yard, and he would make giant dirt caves and he would stay in the caves all day long. Sometimes he would ask me to play in the cave with him, but I never stayed in the dirt for very long.

Carolyn and Constance were identical twin girls, and they really did look just alike. I couldn't tell them apart. They were always together, and they talked alike, they walked alike, and as long as they had each other, they really didn't need anyone else.

My brother Richard was very quiet, he rarely said anything, but when he talked he made everybody laugh. He liked being silly, and that made me giggle, because I liked being silly too.

MeriEllen was only a few years older than me, so we played together all of the time. She was really smart and I learned a lot of things from her. As we played I constantly mimicked what she said, and how she did things. MeriEllen was probably the main reason I learned to talk so early.

Every one of us ran, laughed, and played games together. I knew that I was loved, and that is all that I cared about. Looking through my eyes, I thought we were all the same color; all I could see was my family.

By the time we set out on our journey south, I was getting old enough that I could remember many things that I couldn't have remembered earlier as a baby. I had just turned three years old, and things happened in our travels that I would never forget for as long as I lived.

When we first started on our trip, I loved the adventure of traveling with Aunt Etta, Titus and all of my brothers and sisters and the rest of the families. Each night we would eat food cooked on an open fire pit, and after dinner we sat around the fire and sang gospel hymns. My brothers and sisters and I danced, and sang right along with all of the adults.

Aunt Etta and Titus loved the Lord with all of their hearts, so praising the Lord just came natural to all of us kids. We were continually reminded of how much we had to be thankful for, and after saying our prayers at night we would go to sleep staring up at the magnificent stars. We slept outside on the ground, and I could see the heaven that we had been singing about, and it made me smile.

We had 6 families traveling on our long journey, with three old military mules, and one wagon. We worked together, we ate together, we sang together and everyone helped each other. Many of the older children complained about the long trip, and having to walk every day in the hot sun, or fighting the rain or the blowing winds, but I loved it. Of course, I was still small enough that I often had to be carried by either Titus, Aunt Etta or one of my older brothers or sisters.

I was one of the youngest children in the group. Only one other child named Clarisse was a few months younger than me, so Clarisse was often carried too. We tried to walk, but everyone complained that we waddled too slowly, and it was easier to have us carried on someone's back. Three of the families had received a mule when they had been set free, but not every family had any animals at all.

Our family was one of the first ones to lead the way each day. Titus was large and strong and he was probably what you would call the head of our small group of travelers. We always traveled on back roads staying away from any predominantly white communities. The roads were dusty and narrow and untraveled, but the men thought that we would be safer if we stayed out of sight as much as possible, and we never saw anyone. It had been several years, since any of our families had been in this area, and they did not know what to expect. We were all strangers in an unfamiliar place.

No one in the group had been freed for very long, and they still lived in fear. They especially feared that powerful vigilante group called the Ku

Klux Klan. The Ku Klux Klan did not approve of the black slaves being freed, and our small group of travelers had heard horrible stories of some of the vicious things they had done to other freed black people. The families had been told that the Ku Klux Klan was dissolved, but we had no way of knowing for sure.

Titus felt we would be safer if we stayed away from the larger cities and didn't bring attention to ourselves. None of our group wanted trouble. They just wanted to return back home and live amongst their own people.

The travel each day was slow and tedious. It was late spring and some of the trails that we followed were muddy or flooded from the late spring snow melt in the mountains. We sometimes only traveled just a few miles in a day, because the back roads were rarely used. The farther south we got the more nervous all of the adults became. The adults seemed extra cautious, they often whispered amongst themselves, and they told all of the children not to make any loud noises. I had no idea why we were to be quiet, but to me it was kind of a fun game.

We had been traveling for several days when we came upon an old farmhouse that had been burned to the ground along with all of the outbuildings. Many of the outbuildings were still smoldering, so we knew that the fire had been fairly recent. The men talked quietly and walked around the property looking for the family or for animals, but the property was empty. They seemed relieved that they found no one.

Everyone acted differently after we left the farmhouse behind. Nobody talked, laughed or smiled again. Even the children acted more solemn. We just moved onward keeping a sharp lookout for trouble, although at three years old I didn't even know what trouble looked like, and I wasn't sure if I would recognize trouble if I saw it. But Titus told us to keep a look out, and we always did what Titus said.

The men decided that we were only about fifty miles away from Memphis and the old plantation where all of them had lived and worked before they were freed. They knew the closer we got to Memphis the more dangerous things might become. It was decided that we would camp along the river tonight and set out towards the city in the morning.

That evening we did not start a fire like we usually did. We ate cold beans and leftover bread from the night before. We set up our camp over near a grove of thick trees, and even before dark we were told that we needed to go to sleep.

That night was one of the scariest nights of my life. As I hid silently under my cover trying hard to fall asleep, I could hear animals stomping in the distance. I could feel the pounding of hooves as they got closer and closer to where our group was camping. By the time the animals reached our camp I could tell that something was terribly wrong. At first I was so afraid that I couldn't even move, I was violently shaking all over and I was scared to death. The horses were pawing the ground only a few feet away from where I was trying to sleep.

Next I heard screaming and shouting all around me. Somehow I rolled over and frantically crawled on my hands and knees and hid behind a huge fallen tree, only a few feet away. As I looked out from behind my hiding place, I saw horses snorting, and stomping at the ground and prancing viciously all around my family.

The horses were draped in white sheets and the riders were dressed in white capes from their necks all the way down to their feet. They wore pointed hooded hats with only two small eye holes piercing out from their faces. They placed a cross on the ground in front of Titus and the other men and then they lit the cross on fire before galloping away into the night. There were at least ten or fifteen hooded riders that arrived to frighten us that evening.

I was so terrified that I couldn't move from my hiding place. After the riders left, my sister Mary came looking for me. She put her arms around me and she soothingly comforted me as we held each other and sobbed on each other's shoulders. I could tell that she was just as scared as I was.

Marilynn J. Harris

Early the next morning, all of the adults had a private talk over in the grove apart from the children. It was decided that they needed to take me away to a safer location. They knew that a white child traveling alone with so many black families could cause serious difficulties for all of them. I would create suspicion as to whom I belonged to, and Aunt Etta and Titus had no answers to that question.

After breakfast, all of the families got in a large circle and prayed. My brother Nicolas then walked me around and had me hug everyone before placing me up on one of the mules. I was a compliant child, I wasn't sure what was happening, but I always did as I was told. Nicolas then mounted the mule himself to take me to the safety of the plantation. Aunt Etta retrieved the piece of white paper with my name and birthdate on it that she had been given three years earlier when I was left on her doorstep. She had kept it for me all of these years.

With tears streaming down her face, she placed the piece of paper into the front pocket of Nicolas' shirt and told him, "Give this note to Lady Elizabeth, the lady that lives in the big white house on the plantation where we once lived." She said, "I am sure that baby Harrison will be safe at the plantation, and that Lady Elizabeth will take care of him."

They chose Nicolas to take me because he was the oldest son of Titus and Aunt Etta, and he was almost a full-grown man. The group felt certain that Nicolas and I would make better time if it was just the two of us hastily traveling on the mule.

Titus told Nicolas, "Stay on the back roads, away from any other people. I am sure that you will not have any problems, especially traveling during the daytime hours."

Aunt Etta was crying uncontrollably as she handed me my sleeping blanket, and a straw rag doll that she had made for me when I was younger. I never went anywhere without my ragdoll and blanket, and I couldn't understand what was going on.

I felt confused because Aunt Etta and Titus were the only parents that I had ever known. As I looked at all of the families standing around Nicolas and me, I realized everyone was crying, even the children, so I started to cry too. I knew that something was wrong, but I didn't know what. I wiggled and tried to get down off the mule, but Nicolas held me tightly between his arms, just as he was told to do.

Then he kicked the mule and we were off. No matter how loud I screamed, Nicolas kept right on course heading for the safety of Lady Elizabeth and the big plantation.

Five

Lady Elizabeth

After traveling for several miles on the back of the large mule, I quieted down and stopped screaming and I finally cried myself to sleep holding tightly to my blanket and my ragdoll. When I awoke, we had arrived at the most beautiful place on earth. We slowly rode the mule down the long pathway that led to the front door of a big white mansion. All sides of the driveway were adorned in pleasant pink apple blossom trees. The trees smelled of sweet sugar, the sights and smells were unlike anything I had ever seen or smelled before. The plantation was so peaceful and comforting, I knew it had to be some sort of paradise.

The big white house was about three layers high with windows and verandas and porches off every room. The front of the house had four tall round pillars that went from the ground to the edge of the roof. The front porch was deep, and it was very wide; it extended from one side of the house to other side. The porch was large enough that it had several round tables with numerous chairs placed around each table. It had two painted porch swings, one on each side of the front door.

I was sure this house was as big as the court house where Titus had taken me with him to work. There were flowers and plants placed randomly all throughout the front porch and steps. The whole estate was covered in plush green lawns, wild flowers, and perfectly trimmed hedges.

The closer we got to the house, the more contented I felt. My entire being was at peace. I had never been to such a welcoming place. The bright sunlight filtered down through the trees and spread small glimpses of daylight as we continued on towards the front door of the house.

Nicolas had been raised on this property as a small child. He had lived on this beautiful plantation for much of his life until his family had been freed in 1863, and moved away. He knew the property well, although he had never entered through the front gates before.

When we approached the front of the house an older gentlemen came out to greet us. Nicolas recognized the old man instantly, the man had worked as a slave on this property all of his life, and when he was freed; he had nowhere else to go, so he stayed on to work. Nicolas smiled and hollered out to him, "Hey Charles, It's me Nicolas Lewis, the son of Titus and Etta. I am grown now, and we have come to see Lady Elizabeth."

The old man came over to help Nicolas get down off of the mule and said, "Yes, yes, I recognize you now as I get closer." He nodded his head up and down and said, "You have grown up. You were just boy when all of you moved away several years ago. Now, look at you, you stand much taller than me."

As Nicolas took me down from the mule, I carefully placed my wobbly feet on the ground for the first time in several hours. I was glad to be down off of the animal, and as I turned around I saw the most captivating vision that I had ever seen in my life. I was sure that the lady was one of the majestic angels that Aunt Etta and Titus had told me about. Her hair was an exquisite golden color, and her skin was as white as porcelain. She had sparkling dark blue eyes, and when she smiled at me my heart began to melt.

She wore a long, flowing elegant blue-green dress, and a small feathered matching hat that perfectly accented her brilliant blue eyes. Her lips were a shiny pink color and her cheeks blushed a pale rosy red. Her genuine compassion just radiated out through her entire being as she walked over toward me and knelt down to see my face.

I wanted to cry when she gently brushed my straggly blond curls away from my dirty face and forehead. No one had ever touched me in such a caressing manner before. I just stared intently into her beautiful face; I could hardly breathe. While she was standing so close to me I realized she smelled wonderful, like fresh flowers and clean soap.

"Who is this handsome young man?" she softly asked still smiling, and staring directly into my eyes.

Nicolas instantly recognized the stunning fair-skinned lady of the house. She was Lady Elizabeth, the person we had been sent here to see. Of course Nicolas was nervous as he spoke to the enchanting woman, although he knew her; he had never talked to her before. He shyly put his head down and rapidly began telling her why we had come, he said, "Lady Elizabeth, my name is Nicolas. I am the son of Titus and Etta Lewis, and this young man is Harrison Obadiah Pike." Nicolas quickly pulled the white piece of paper from his pocket, and handed it to Lady Elizabeth.

As she read the paper, she noticed it was written in a woman's handwriting. She questionably stared at the piece of paper for a few seconds because all that the note said was,

Harrison Obadiah Pike   April 16, 1867.

She looked up from the note and gently asked Nicolas, "I don't understand. What does this note mean, and how did you get this child?"

Nicolas explained, "My mother was working as a wet nurse to help newborn babies. The child was left with my mother to care for as an infant, and no one ever returned to get him." Nicolas went on, "He has been with our family for three years. When we decided to move back home we had no choice but to bring him with us, because he had nowhere else to go."

Nicolas glanced back over to where I was patiently standing and then he went on, "Last night our camp was visited by a group of the Ku Klux Klan members on horseback. The visitors did not see Harrison at that time, because it was very dark and he was hidden in the trees." Nicolas closed his eyes and let out a big sigh before he continued, "We all fear what might happen if they return and discover a young white child traveling with a community of black families."

He went on to say, "No one outside of our black community has ever seen young Harrison in the three years that he has been living with our family. A few weeks ago we decided to pack all of our belongings, and come back to the south. We have returned to find work, and to live amongst our family members." Nicolas covered his face with his hands and continued, "My mother thought you might help the young child, because baby Harrison has no one."

This was the first time that I had ever heard how I got to be in Aunt Etta's family. No one had ever told me any of my story before. A child only knows what he has been taught, and what he has lived through, and all that I had ever known was Aunt Etta, Titus and their family. It wasn't until that moment when I heard Nicolas telling Lady Elizabeth about me, that I realized I was all alone. I could no longer live with Aunt Etta's family anymore, so I really didn't belong anywhere.

Lady Elizabeth seemed very touched by the genuine feelings that Nicolas shared for me. She told me later that she could not believe that they had cared enough about me to take me to the wet nurse so that I would not die, yet they did not care enough to come back to get me or even check on me.

As she studied both Nicolas and me, she smiled, because Nicolas treated me like a real brother. The beautiful lady needed some time to think about all of this, so before giving him an answer, she smiled and gently touched Nicolas's hand and said, "I'll bet you and the young child are hungry and thirsty from your long journey." She motioned for Charles to bring me to the house so we could all go in and get something to eat.

Nicolas was hesitant to walk up to the front porch. This was something abnormal for him, he hesitated and just couldn't do it. He had always lived in the back, in the slave quarters. As he approached the steps he shook his head back and forth and said, "I'm sorry Lady Elizabeth, but I'd better stay right out here."

Lady Elizabeth looked at his face, and she understood. "Well, that would be just fine," she said. "Why don't you and the child go wash up over by the pond and I'll have Maddie fix us up something cool to drink and some nice sandwiches, and then we can all talk."

As Nicolas and I went around to the side of the house to do our business, and to wash up in the pond, Lady Elizabeth walked on into the house to have the food prepared. As soon as she closed the front door behind her, she gently wiped back the tears that were escaping down her beautiful face. She silently said to herself, "Of course I will take this precious child that God has sent to me."

Then she quietly prayed a prayer of thanksgiving as she stood there weeping, because she had been reverently asking the Lord to somehow send her a child of her own. Lady Elizabeth had been married to her husband Andrew for over ten years, yet she was childless. She had been pregnant many times, but each time she had been unable to carry the pregnancies to full term. After she lost her latest baby five months ago, the doctor warned her of the dangers about getting pregnant again.

Lady Elizabeth had stayed in bed the entire pregnancy, just as the doctor had told her to do. But, no matter how hard she tried to keep healthy, she had no appetite and she could not gain weight. Finally, the precious newborn was just too tiny to survive, and three weeks before the infant was due, she once again miscarried. It was a baby boy.

A few days after the dead baby was delivered the doctor told both her and her husband, "I am so sorry; I know how much you want children, but this pregnancy has to be your last attempt. The risk is too high. If you get pregnant again I'm sure neither you, nor the new baby will survive."

The doctor's information devastated the couple, because he was telling them that they would never have a family. For days after she lost that baby, Lady Elizabeth just remained in her room, and stared out her bedroom window. She struggled to eat or talk to anyone. When a woman is pregnant and loses a baby, her arms are empty, and she can think of nothing else except having a child to fill that emptiness.

She and her husband had been praying diligently for the Lord to allow them to have children, and then the doctor told them there was absolutely no hope. Now, only a few months after the loss of their last baby, this beautiful young boy had been sent to them, and he has no family.

She felt like leaping for joy, she knew the child had to be a direct answer to all of their prayers. She giggled to herself as she thought of the unique way the Lord had put together her request and she quietly whispered, "In all of the hours that I reverently prayed, I never imagined that the child would be a handsome three year old boy with long blond curls, riding up on a mule." She then covered her face and could no longer hold back the tears of delight as she said to herself, "And he even looks like me."

Throughout the afternoon Nicolas and Lady Elizabeth talked and she observed the way I behaved, I was very quiet and polite. She told me months later that she had been so impressed by the way Nicolas treated me; she knew he truly loved me as his brother, and that made her love me even more.

She told Nicolas, "There is a plantation about seventy-five miles south of here that would probably hire all of the families in your group and you would be safe there." She wrote a letter to the plantation owner for Nicolas to take with him to give to the owner so that the families could find work.

Marilynn J. Harris

She also told him, "I am quite sure the Ku Klux Klan will not bother you there."

That night Nicolas and I slept out in the barn with soft blankets and fresh piles of hay. It had been a long day and I was exhausted, but I knew that Nicolas would be leaving me in the morning, so I had a very difficult time sleeping. I snuggled with my blanket and ragdoll, however, so many things had changed in my world in the past few weeks that I couldn't go to sleep. Images of the scary men on horses kept racing through my mind, and I could still see Aunt Etta crying as we rode away on the mule. I finally calmed down holding tightly to my brother's arm, and fell sound asleep until morning.

Early the next morning, we had breakfast with Lady Elizabeth out on the lawn. We ate eggs, ham and warm biscuits with honey, and as soon as we were finished eating, Nicolas stood up and hugged me goodbye. He told Lady Elizabeth thank you and he climbed back on the old mule that we had arrived on the day before, and he turned the mule and just briskly walked away down the lane.

This time I didn't cry. I just stood there silently watching Nicolas until he was completely out of sight. He never once turned around to look at me, he just kept on going. Nicolas had talked to me the night before when we were going to sleep in the barn. He said, "We each have a job to do, and my first job was to bring you here and then return to my family, and go with them and find work." He told me, "Your job is to be brave after I'm gone, and stay here with Lady Elizabeth."

I tried to be brave and do my job as I continued to stand there, but I was only three years old and I didn't know what to do. I wasn't sure how to act brave. I had never been without Nicolas, Aunt Etta, Titus and my other brothers and sisters before.

I was in deep thought when I felt the soft hand of Lady Elizabeth touch my shoulder. I turned and looked into her face, and I could no longer be brave or hold back the horrendous feeling of abandonment that was inside of me. The beautiful lady held out her arms, and I instantly ran to her and uncontrollably wailed.

As I cried on her shoulder, Lady Elizabeth picked me up in her arms and hugged me tighter than I had ever been hugged before, and she cried too. It felt so good to be comforted, I had never felt such genuine love. I was just a little boy, and my world seemed so confused. As I snuggled on her shoulder she carried me up the front steps to go into the house to meet my new father, Andrew Thomas Langley II.

My head popped up from Lady Elizabeth's shoulder when I realized I was entering the front door of the mansion. I wiped my eyes, and all thoughts of crying disappeared as I gazed around at the stately dwelling. The front area was adorned in brightly colored Persian rugs and red velvet chairs. The ceilings were high with several huge dangling crystal candle chandeliers hanging down from the tall ceilings.

The front-room area was vast, and it had bright beaming sunshine streaming in through the glistening tall windows. Each window was draped in heavy velvet maroon drapes that were pulled back to let the happiness of the morning sun smile through. Dainty white lace curtains covered the tall majestic windows under each set of draperies.

The room was decorated with countless dark oak side board tables with numerous drawers for linens and serving utensils. The tables were shined and polished to a bright luster, and several tables were skirted in crisp white linen table covers, and every table had fresh flowers in brightly colored vases. Many tables held candle lamps with painted glass covers. Each lamp cover was hand painted with bright roses or dainty yellow daisies. The room was decorated with all of the most modern attributes and conveniences of that period.

The walls held several large pictures of soldiers from the war, or men with white hair posing sophisticated looking, with one hand in their coat pocket, and smugly gazing to the side.

Marilynn J. Harris

Some of the portraits were of beautiful ladies, in colorful long dresses with large feathered hats. Each one sat gracefully in a straight-back chair, tilting her head to one side with her nose in the air, trying to look refined. None of the people in the portraits looked very happy, because no one was smiling.

Lady Elizabeth carried me straight ahead through a doorway and into a large dining room. This room held a long mahogany table with several formal dining room chairs lined up along each side of the table. It had one enormous French-cut glass candle chandelier hanging directly in the center of the room, suspended down and encompassing a large portion of the formal dining room table. Sitting at the far end of the table was a tall slender man with thick dark hair, and striking dark blue eyes.

I did not know it at the time, but the man was anxious to meet me. He had watched me from one of the upstairs windows the day before when I was outside with Nicolas and Lady Elizabeth. Also, he and Lady Elizabeth had talked about me for several hours the night before, after Nicolas and I went out to the barn to go to bed.

Lady Elizabeth had explained my full story to him, and I soon discovered that he too felt that I was an answer to their prayers. They had both earnestly prayed for a child, and I belonged to no one. I was told years later that although he had never even seen me up close until that moment; he had already accepted me to be his chosen son, and an heir to his family heritage.

Lady Elizabeth slowly placed me down on the floor next to where the man was sitting, finishing up his breakfast, and she stated, "Andrew, this young man is Harrison." She put her hands on my shoulders and bent over the side of me and said, "Harrison, this is the man of the house, my husband, Andrew Langley."

I just stood there staring at the gentleman. I had never seen a man with such light skin before, and I wasn't sure what I was supposed to do. But I wasn't crying so I knew I was doing my job and being brave.

44

Before anyone could say anything else, the cook named Maddie came in to pick up the dishes. I smiled a huge smile and almost ran to her, because she looked a lot like Aunt Etta. For one brief second I thought Aunt Etta had come back for me, but I was wrong.

The man of the house then spoke so that I would turn back around and look at him. He seemed absolutely delighted as he smiled at me and said, "Harrison do you like lollies?"

I had no idea what he was talking about. I did not know what a lollie was, so I didn't know if I liked them or not. I wasn't sure what to answer, but the nice man seemed so cheerful that I wasn't the least bit afraid of him. I remained silent just staring at him. I was thinking quietly to myself, "Lollies must be something very special, or he wouldn't be smiling such a big smile as he talked about them."

As I stood there trying to figure out what to do, Lady Elizabeth once again put her hands on my shoulders and said, "Andrew, I don't know if Harrison has ever eaten a lollie." She then motioned for the lady that looked like Aunt Etta to go and get me a lollie to eat.

Within minutes the lady returned with a tray full of lollies, and walked over to the man of the house and placed them on the table. The man then motioned for me to move closer to him so that I could choose which lollie I wanted.

As I gazed down on the tray full of colorful sugar sticks, I first grabbed a red stick and slowly put the candy into my mouth. After tasting the delicious sweet candy, I quickly picked up a bright yellow candy too, so that I had a lollie in each hand. For some strange reason both Lady Elizabeth, and the man of the house burst out laughing when I chose two sticks at one time.

Lady Elizabeth instantly put her arms around me and squeezed me tight and said, "Oh Harrison you are such a delight." She smiled at me and said, "You are such a smart, handsome young man"

"Yes, yes you are a brilliant boy," said the man of the house as he cheerfully laughed out loud and grinned from ear to ear.

I just stood there first licking the red candy and then the yellow, and I couldn't help it, I smiled too. No one had ever given me any attention like this before, and I had never been told that I was brilliant. I liked these people.

The man of the house stood up and walked over to me. He was tall, but he squatted down on one knee so that he could talk to me face to face. He said, "Harrison do you like ponies, I think we need to choose a pony for you to have as your very own."

I smiled at the man as he looked into my face, I couldn't help it; I felt so comfortable. Lady Elizabeth and this nice man just kept talking to me as if I was someone important. I was so glad that Nicolas had brought me to these people.

"First he needs a haircut, a bath and some clean clothes," Lady Elizabeth said as she led me to another area of the house. "Then you can chose a pony," she giggled as she walked away still talking to the man of the house as he stood there watching us.

Within a few minutes, an older gentleman with white hair came into the room where she had taken me. He came in to cut off my long golden locks, and when he was done I could see large clumps of blond curls covering the floor all around the chair. I had never had a haircut before.

Soon a lady brought me a crisp white shirt, and a new pair of trousers that she had just sewn for me. These were the first new clothes I had ever had. All I had ever worn before was something that one of Aunt Etta's children had outgrown, or a neighbor in the black community had given me.

After my bath, Lady Elizabeth combed my hair and dressed me in my new clothes. She then walked me over to a full length reflection mirror and I saw myself in a mirror for the first time in my life. I looked first at the mirror, and then back behind me, I couldn't figure out why things in the mirror were the same as they were all around.

Lady Elizabeth stood next to me and bent down so that our cheeks were touching as we both looked at ourselves side by side in the mirror. My skin was just like hers. My hair was almost the same golden blond color as hers, and our eyes were both the same dark shade of blue.

I turned to look directly at her beautiful face, and she had tears running down her soft cheeks. I smiled and she closed her eyes, and softly kissed my forehead. I just stared at her and smiled, because no one had ever kissed me before, and I liked it.

Lady Elizabeth took my hand and led me back towards the parlor area where Andrew Langley was patiently waiting for me to get cleaned up. When we approached him, he stood up and said, "What a handsome young man you are after a bath and a haircut." He put his hand out for me to hold onto, and the three of us walked hand in hand out the front door and down the steps to the yard.

As we walked, Lady Elizabeth and the man of the house just talked and laughed like this was a walk we had done many times before. I looked up at her and then up at him. My heart was so full of joy I thought it might burst. I smiled the biggest smile that I could possibly smile. I had never been so happy in my life. I liked holding hands and taking walks, and thankfully this was just the first of many walks I would take with this new family.

We walked out to the hay fields and then down a long lane to where a tall white fence enclosed several beautiful thoroughbred horses. The man picked me up, and put me up on the top rail of the fence so that I could look at the horses better. He said, "See all of the horses, they belong to us, we have over thirty thoroughbreds."

I was absolutely in awe as I watched the horses grazing out in the fields. They were much thinner, and so much more graceful than the mules that I had seen before. Because I was still so young, my new parents had no idea how well I could talk, but actually I could speak very well. I talked with a strong black southern brogue, like Aunt Etta and Titus and all of my older brothers and sisters, but I talked in complete sentences. And thanks to my sister MeriEllen, I could say almost anything.

I had been very quiet all the time we had been walking, I just listened to them talk and I grinned a lot, but I never said a word. So, when I spoke for the first time, my new father just stared at me in amazement and beamed. He lightly tilted his head in towards my forehead and grinned, as I sat proudly on the fence with one arm wrapped tightly around his shoulder. He quietly said, "You really are a brilliant young man." Then he hugged me even tighter than he had before, and he gently whispered to me with tears in his eyes, "I have waited for so many years to have a son. I can't believe that after all of my prayers, you are really here, and you are not only handsome, but you are also unbelievably smart."

I had no idea until that moment that these magnificent people were planning to keep me, and be my parents. Lady Elizabeth was so gracious and beautiful, and Andrew Langley was such an easy man to like. He was kind, honest and gentle, and I soon learned that he desperately wanted to be my father; almost as much as I wanted to be his son. I never realized how much I had missed in my life, until I came to live with my new parents. They genuinely loved me, and needed me. The Lord had chosen such wonderful people to be my parents, and I think I loved them from the very first day.

After strolling throughout the massive property, we returned to the house to have a light lunch and tea. My new parents made me my own special place at the table with china plates, sparkling silverware, linen napkins, and a crystal water goblet. It was my permanent place of belonging. It is the exact same place that I used every day from that day on while growing up in the big white house.

I had never seen such beautiful dishes before, but I soon got used to using shiny silverware and china plates. Even when I would spill my water glass all over the elegant table, my parents did not get angry with me. They just continued to teach me until I learned to eat like a gentleman.

Many things just came natural to me when I came to live with my new family, but sleeping all alone in my own bedroom, was not one of those natural things. It was terrifying for me. I had never slept in a bed alone; let alone in a room by myself. I had always been in a large room with several other children sleeping all around me.

In Aunt Etta's family the boys slept in one large bed, and the girls slept in two other beds, but all of us were in the same room, so I was never alone. My entire life, up until that time, I always had lots of people around me wherever I went. It seemed very abnormal to be all by myself. I didn't know how to act.

As I knelt beside my new bed that first night with my brand-new mother and father by my side, I prayed for all of Aunt Etta's family, and for all of the other families in their group. I prayed for the Lord to keep them safe from the scary men on horses, and I prayed for Nicolas to be brave, so that he could do his job too.

Aunt Etta had taught me to pray as soon I learned to talk. Praying was just a natural form of talking to the Lord for me, and she taught me to always be thankful. So, as I prayed in my new house that first evening, I thanked the Lord for the beautiful Lady Elizabeth and for the man of the house, Andrew Langley. I also innocently thanked the Lord that we could all hold hands, and take a walk and see the horses. That was such a special time for me.

Both Lady Elizabeth and Andrew Langley leaned over and kissed me goodnight. They pulled the covers up under my chin as they prepared to leave me alone in the dark. The bed was big and soft with fluffy clean covers, but I still was afraid to be by myself.

I stayed there, all alone in the dark for several minutes staring up at the ceiling. The moon was shining in through the bedroom window, and it made shadows that looked like giant dancing monsters jumping around throughout the big room. I pulled the covers up around my face until I could barely see out through only one tiny space, but I didn't cry or climb out of bed. I just remained there quietly trying to do my job and be brave.

I don't know how long I had been there with my eyes wide open before Lady Elizabeth tiptoed into my room with my blanket and my rag doll. When I realized she was there, I sat up and wrapped my arms around her neck and wouldn't let her leave.

"Oh my precious, precious little man," she muttered as she rocked me tightly in her arms. She whispered softly with her cheek up next to mine, "Are you scared of the dark?" I just clung to her, and nodded my head up and down, but said nothing.

"Don't be afraid my little one, I'm here and I promise I won't ever leave you; everything will be alright from now on," she reassured me still holding me in her arms. As she gently rocked me back and forth on my new bed, she softly sang this Christian hymn to me: "*Shall we gather at the river, where bright angel feet have trod, with the crystal tide forever, flowing by the throne of God. Yes, we'll gather at the river, the beautiful, the beautiful river, gather with the saints at the river; that flows by the throne of God.*"

The song about the river was one of the hymns that Aunt Etta and Titus and all of the black families sang each night, as we assembled around the campfire. I listened closely as Lady Elizabeth sang to me, it was comforting, because it was a song that I knew.

The song of the river had been one of Aunt Etta's favorite songs. "Shall We Gather at the River" was a fairly new hymn at that time. It was written a few years earlier by a Baptist minister by the name of Robert Lowry.

I loved that song, and I loved to hear my mother sing it to me. She sang the 'song of the river' to me every night, after I said my prayers. It helped me to fall asleep. As she sang to me, I pictured a peaceful river where the saints like Aunt Etta and Titus, and my brothers and sisters gathered to praise the Lord.

****

I had lived with my new parents for almost a month when they got me my first pony. Even though I was only three years old, my parents let me name my pony any name that I wanted to. My mom suggested Goldie or Prince. My dad said Thunder, Champion or Blaze, but as I stood there and studied my beautiful new mount, I realized that the most meaningful thing in my life was the river song that my mother sang to me each evening. So, as silly as it might have sounded, I called my pony…Song of the River. Because no matter how much I loved my new parents, and my new home, my heart and thoughts mourned for the loss of Aunt Etta, Titus and my brothers and sisters. The song of the river that my mother sang to me, helped tie all of us together as a family.

My pony, 'River' was my pride and joy. He was the first thing in my life that really belonged to me. I had my rag doll and my blanket, but River was different; he was more like a companion. He was sleek, graceful and beautiful and he loved to eat carrots right out of my hand. I was so proud of him. His beautiful mane and tail seemed to float, and bounce as he pranced up and down the driveway. I often wished I could show River to Nicolas and my other brothers and sisters. I know they would have loved him too. My pony was so gentle that he would let me climb all over him without kicking, nipping me or even moving. He was very well trained, and my mom and dad trusted him completely.

They did not put River out in the big field like they did all of the other horses. They wanted him nearby so that I could ride him every day. He stayed in the barn behind the house. It was the same barn that Nicolas and I slept in the first night that we arrived at the plantation.

51

Marilynn J. Harris

River was a small palomino quarter horse that my parents had purchased from a quarter horse ranch several miles away. They decided on a small horse rather than a child's pony so that I wouldn't outgrow him in a few years. Also, ponies can be kind of mischievous at times, and well-bred horses are a little more predictable.

I had my own saddle that was just my size, and my father would lead River and me up and down the driveway many times each day until I got tired, and I was ready to get off. I brushed him, petted him, and when he would put his head down, I could spread my arms across his head, and hug his entire face. I saw River every day, and I loved him with my entire being, but my parents were still very protective, and very wise. For the first few months, they never let me handle River alone. I was still really young and they wouldn't let me hold the reins until I got older, and had learned to ride better.

My pony was an eye-catching dark palomino with a perfect white marking on his face that ran from the top of his head down between his eyes and blended into his muzzle. He had a double thick golden-white mane that parted down the middle and fell equally on both sides of his neck, and flopped down his face partially covering his eyes. His tail was a matching golden-white color that fell to the ground and swept upward at the bottom when he walked. His mane and tail were almost the exact color of my own blonde curls.

He had two perfectly matched white socks that went a third of the way up his front legs, and he was absolutely beautiful. Having real parents that loved me, and having my very own pony truly did make my home a paradise.

Six weeks after I arrived at the big white house my father had a lawyer draw up a legal name-change for me. He wanted to make me his real son as soon as possible. With no family members to contact, and no one to contest my name-change, everything took effect as soon as the papers were signed. My new name became Harrison Andrew Langley, after my father.

They left my first name Harrison and everyone called me Harry. From that day on I called Lady Elizabeth, my mom and Andrew Langley, my dad.

Six

A Train Ride to Chicago

I had been with my new family for over a year when there was a huge fire in the city of Chicago about 550 miles away. My parents were very disturbed because they had relatives that still lived in Chicago. My mother had been born there, and she had left all of her family behind when she married my father Andrew Langley, and moved with him to Tennessee. My parents received word that thousands of people had lost their homes, and several people had died.

My mother's family had sent her a newspaper article telling all about the terrible fire. The article said that the fire had started at about 9:00 p.m. on October 8, 1871 on a small farm owned by the O'Leary family of 137 DeKoven Street. Many people believed that the fire ignited when Mrs. O'Leary's cow kicked over a lantern as it was being milked out in the barn. The shed next to the barn was the first to be consumed by the fire. Strong southwest winds carried flying embers towards the heart of the city.

The article stated that in those days more than two-thirds of the town's structures were made out of wood. All of the sidewalks and even many of the roads were also made of wood. Also, Chicago had only received an inch of rain from July to October causing a severe drought throughout the region. 185 firemen and 17 horse-drawn steam engines were all that they had to protect the entire city.

It was suggested that another reason the fire got so far out of control was that the watchman for the fire department sent the firefighters to the wrong place and that turned a small fire into a conflagration. When the firemen finally arrived at DeKoven Street, the fire had grown and spread to neighboring buildings, and was already progressing to the central business district.

The fire engulfed the lumber yard and the coal yard around 11:30 p.m. The flames and debris blew across the river and landed on roofs, and the South Side Gas Works. When the courthouse caught fire, the mayor ordered all of the prisoners released from the basement. At 2:20 the courthouse roof collapsed sending the great bell crashing down through the destroyed structure, falling all the way to the ground below.

Some people believed that there was also a meteorological phenomenon known at that time as a fire whirl. It is when over-heated air rises and comes in contact with cooler air and it begins to spin creating a tornado like effect. It was these whirls that drove flames across the Chicago River to a railroad car filled with kerosene.

After the fire jumped the river, a burning piece of timber lodged on the roof of the city's Waterworks building and destroyed that building, the water went dry and the city was helpless. The fire then burned from building to building, and from block to block.

Finally, on October 9th it started to rain, but even after the fire was out the burned city smoldered for several days. Eventually, it was determined that the fire destroyed an area of about 4 miles long and three-fourths of a mile wide; about 2,000 acres. It burned 73 miles of roads, 120 miles of sidewalk, 2, 000 lampposts, 17,500 buildings and $222 million dollars in property. Of the 300,000 inhabitants 100,000 were left homeless. 120 bodies were recovered, but the death toll may have been as high as 300. The county coroner said it was hard to get an exact count because some may have drowned in the river, or they could have been incinerated leaving no remains. The Chicago fire would go down in history as one of the worst fire disasters of all time.

Even though Chicago was hundreds of miles away from Memphis, my mother agonized over the loss of her beautiful city. I had never seen Chicago or any of the family members that lived there, but the horrible fire devastated both of my parents. They loved Chicago; that is where they had first met.

Although none of our relatives had died in the fire, they had all lost their homes. My mother was so upset that she wanted to take the train and go back to Chicago as soon as she received word that the fire was out.

My father calmly told her, "No, let's wait awhile and give the people of the city some time to clean up and rebuild. They have been through a horrendous calamity, and there is nothing we can do to help them right now. I'm sure most of the people of the city are completely overwhelmed, but I will send our relatives money to help them with whatever they need."

He then glanced over at me with a loving smile on his face before stating, "Also, you wouldn't want to travel without Harry, and you don't want to go now and take our son into the middle of all of that devastation." My wise father went on, "If we wait awhile then all three of us can take the train and travel to Chicago together. We have not been back for over two years, it is time for us to take Harry for a visit anyway. Even traveling by train it will be a very long trip; so when we go I will arrange for us to stay for several months."

My mother quickly shook her head up and down and then buried her face into my father's shoulder and agreed, "You're right, this would not be a good time to go. We'll wait until we hear that things are a little more settled." She then walked over towards the window and covered her face with her hands before saying, "I just wish there was something I could do. I feel so helpless being so far away."

"I know, I feel helpless too," My father said as he walked over behind her and put his hands on her shoulders to reassure her that things would be alright. He gently leaned around her right side, and kissed her on the cheek.

He said to her, "Now come over to the table and sit down and I will pour you a cup of hot tea. It will make you feel better."

I loved to watch the unpretentious kindness that my father and mother showed for each other. As a child, I probably learned more from watching them together, than I did from anything else that I was taught throughout my lifetime.

My mother sat down for her tea and smiled, then she said to my father "You're right, tea always makes me feel better." Then she motioned for me to come to her open arms, and as she hugged me and said, "Oh Harry, I just love you so much, your father is right. I could never take the trip without you, and I would never take you someplace that you would not be safe, so we will wait and we can all go together. You will like riding on the train," she said as she hugged me tight and kissed me on my forehead.

My mother waited patiently each day to hear from her family. She finally got a letter from her sister in Chicago stating that their father was not doing well. Her sister Charlotte told her, "Father has developed a severe cough after working in the rubble during the fire clean-up. The family property is at the center of the worst devastation, and Father had been laboring endlessly to clear the destruction and rebuild the house. As a result, he developed severe breathing problems." She went on, "He has been put in the hospital and the doctors do not know if he will recover." She stated, "His condition seems to be getting worse every day. His situation has become even graver over the past few days."

Marilynn J. Harris

After reading the letter my mother urgently exclaimed, "It is time for us to go." Actually she had been ready for weeks, so the three of us finished packing up our belongings, took the buckboard carriage, and headed for the train station to go to Chicago. The station was about twenty miles away in Memphis.

That was the first time that I had ever traveled on a train. My family usually stayed fairly close to the plantation, and I had only been into the city of Memphis twice since I had arrived at the big white house last year. My father's parents lived in Memphis, so I went to visit them on two different occasions, but they usually came and stayed at the plantation with us. They lived in a big brick house right on Main Street. The first time that I went there was when the lawyer did the papers for my name to be changed. My father was so proud to call me his son that he took me to Memphis to meet my new grandparents, the day after the papers were signed.

My father often traveled on business and he would be gone for several days at a time, but I always stayed at home with my mother. I was excited about our journey, because this would be a new adventure for me to travel all the way from Tennessee to Illinois.

When we arrived at the train station, my family unloaded our bags and walked up onto the large planked station platform to wait for the train. I waved goodbye to Charles as he left us at the station, and he drove away in the buckboard to head back to the plantation. I quickly found a place and sat down on a hard wooden bench that was placed up against the train station wall. My mother sat down beside me as my father got our tickets at the station window.

The man in the window said the train would arrive in around thirty minutes. I sat quietly on the wooden bench anxiously watching down the train track, afraid to take my eyes away from that direction. It looked like the tracks went on forever. I had never seen a train before, so I was so excited that could hardly wait. My dad had shown me pictures of a train, in a picture book that he had brought for me on one of his business trips, but as the train approached the station I could not believe that it was even bigger than I had ever imagined.

I was absolutely in awe of the giant train. I was so captivated that even after the train came to a complete stop, I couldn't move. In fact, I was a little intimidated. It wasn't until my dad reached for my hand and said, "Hey, are you coming with us?" That I got up and walked hesitantly to the train steps. I couldn't take my eyes off of the white puffs that appeared to be floating out all sides of the giant train engine.

As I scrutinized the giant monster, I couldn't decide if I should run up the stairs to enter the train car with my parents, or take off running in a different direction to get away from the powerful, noisy contraption. I looked up at my father and he was grinning from ear to ear. He wasn't the least bit afraid of the giant train. Then I looked up at my mother's face and she was lovingly smiling down at me, and I could tell that she wasn't afraid of the boisterous train either. So, I took a deep breath and cautiously climbed the stairs to enter the doors of the quivering monster; we entered the belly of the beast, and looked for a place to sit down.

The inside of the train was beautiful. The seats were made of a dark golden velvet and the ceilings and sides were covered in the same matching velvet material. There were people sitting in almost every seat. They all looked happy, and each person smiled at us and said hello as we walked by. As I rapidly glanced around, I noticed that none of the people seemed frightened of riding the train, so I tried to not be afraid either, but the train was so...ominous.

Even before the train started to move, my father scooted me over by the window and said, "Here Harry you will want to sit by the window so you can watch everything as it goes by." My mother sat in the seats facing us and she smiled at me as I clung tightly to my father's hand and wouldn't let go.

A man in a black coat came by to collect our tickets, and within minutes the train kind of bucked and jumped, and started to move. I just stared out the big windows as the train began to speed up, but I never let go of my father's hand. I was absolutely mesmerized as the train started surging down the tracks. Riding on the train and watching out of the big open window was unlike anything I had ever experienced before.

The train traveled faster than I had ever gone in my life. It was so unbelievable that I just sat at the window staring out at the dashing trees, bridges and buildings as we raced by them heading for Chicago. I couldn't imagine how anything could move so quickly. I had ridden in the buckboard, and I had trotted on my horse, River. I had even ridden on a mule, but nothing compared to the excitement of speeding down the tracks in this giant moving machine.

Traveling on the train opened a whole new world for me. We crossed tall bridges and rushed past miles and miles of corn fields. I gazed at giant buildings as we went through big cities and I watched in awe as we passed through the train yards in the larger areas. My life had been so sheltered until now, I had never been exposed to so much action. There were hundreds of people everywhere.

We often stopped at train stations as we passed through the towns. Sometimes people would be waiting at the station to get on our train car when we stopped, and sometimes people that had been riding with us got off when the train pulled into the station.

I soon got used to the train wheels skidding and grinding to get started again after each time we stopped. We traveled over high train trestles that left the river flowing methodically far below us. I contentedly sat and stared out the window as the miles flew by. I saw fields of open pastures filled with cows, horses and acres of wild flowers.

As we went through cities, I could see children playing in a park, and people walking their dogs. I saw things from my train window that I never knew existed, there were new things to see everywhere I looked.

On the second day of our trip, one of the men wearing a black jacket came by our train seats and secretly whispered something into my father's ear. Whatever the man had whispered to my father made him smile a huge smile, because he shook his head up and down and stated, "Oh my son Harry would love that."

I perked up at the sound of my name and shyly said, "What Father? What would I love?"

My father leaned over so that only my mother and I could hear him and he quietly whispered, "The conductor wanted to know if we would like to go up to the front of the train and meet the engineer when the train stops. I told him I thought you would like that, wouldn't you Harry?"

I jumped up and down in my train seat and rapidly tapped on my father's arm and said, "Oh could we Father, could we please."

My parents and I had walked around to see several of the other train cars, but we had never gone up to the front area of the train. I had been to the dining car when we ate, and we had passed through several other passenger cars and then to the back of the train where the caboose rode.

We had walked over the walkway numerous times that connected the cars together, and I was beginning to feel quite daring. At first it really scared me walking outside to cross the wobbly plank to get to the other train cars, but we had done it several times since we first got on the train. I was becoming pretty bold, as long as I could hold tight to my father's hand.

I was beginning to love everything about riding the train, and now I was even going to the front of the train to see the engineer, I was ecstatic.

At the next train station, as soon as the train came to a complete stop, my father and I hopped off the train and walked up to the engine. My father quickly lifted me up to enter the huge steam engine. This was a long station stop and we were told that we would have time to talk to the engineer before the train needed to leave the station.

My father shook hands with the engineer and told him, "Good afternoon my name is Andrew Langley and this is my son Harry. Thank you for allowing Harry and me to come up front to the engine area." My father looked down at me and beamed as he stated, "This is my son's very first train trip, and he is so excited to meet you."

The locomotive engineer reached out his hand to shake my hand and said, "Well, hello Harry my name is engineer Roger. I am the person who drives the train, and this is fireman Darrell," he said pointing to the man next to him. Darrell just nodded hello, and kept on working. "Fireman Darrell is the person in charge of keeping the train fueled and running." Both engineer Roger and fireman Darrell wore blue thin-striped jumpsuits, and a light colored cap.

The inside of the engine was filled with sticks and levers and even as we talked Roger kept his hand upon the throttle. I was in awe of everything about the train, so I timidly asked the engineer, "How do you get to be a locomotive engineer?"

Within a few seconds Roger began to relax and he turned around and talked to me about how a person learns to drive a train. He said, "Being an engineer is a job of action, the engineer must be alert at all times, because a steam locomotive is full of energy and strength. The trains of today can travel up to 60 miles per hour. You must be able to keep your eyes upon the rail at all times."

He told us, "Up until the last two years most train lines were still quite primitive and they used scrap rail, namely metal plate that was put on top of a wooden rail. It was much cheaper to make, but lousy for smoothness and speed." He continued, "The train could only go 20 or 30 miles per hour, and the ride was really rough. Now with the newer, stronger steel rails both in the South and in the North we can travel up to 60 miles per hour with a much smoother ride."

He continued, "Most locomotive engineers know how each part of the train works, so if there is a problem we can correct the situation. Most engineers start out as a machinist's or broiler maker's apprentice."

Roger went on, "The second job might be to work in a shop or round house where locomotives are repaired. Next he might be a hostler; a person who runs the locomotives around the shops and repair yards." He said, "Then he might become a locomotive fireman. The fireman's job furnishes the final training ground for the job of the engineer."

He went on, "Every locomotive engineer is selected from the ranks of fireman. His first job is running and switching the train cars around, and pushing and pulling cars back and forth in the railroad yards."

Engineer Roger smiled, "It is every boy's dream to become a locomotive engineer, and I love telling children about trains." He continued, "The next step is to be assigned to a local freight run, and finally as he gains experience and seniority he gets a long distance freight passenger run. Engineers work day and night, for the railroads never sleep." He went on, "Trains must be kept running at all times. Engineers must be of sound mind and have good eyesight. He must be alert, dependable and trustworthy. The punctual operation and safety of passengers and express mail and freight depend upon the reliability and intelligence of those who operate the trains."

He told us, "The engineer must pass a difficult examination to prove that he is thoroughly familiar with the technical details of locomotive operation. Every engineer must have a physical examination periodically, and he must be off duty at least 8 hours in a row before getting back in the engineer position on the train."

Roger then showed us where the engineer sits behind the boiler and firebox. "That area contains all of the controls and manual gauges, and indicators on how the locomotive is performing." He told us, "To start the engine the engineer releases the air brake and pulls the throttle slowly towards him. To stop he applies the brakes and moves the throttle in the other direction."

He showed us that the lever with the little black spot in the center controls the air brakes and that controls the entire length of the train. "Just above the engineer is a whistle cord which signals the crew." He told us, "Two pulls on the cord signals the train will start moving. While stopped three short pulls means backing up, and 4 short pulls releases the brakes. When the train is in motion, three short pulls signals to stop at the next station. One short pull and one long pull means to inspect the train. One long pull and one short pull means the visibility is obscured." Engineer Roger told us, "While the train is moving multiple short pulls in a row signals there is danger, or something needs to get off of the track. We oftentimes are forced to shoot buffalo, or other large animals right from the train window if they will not clear the tracks."

It was almost time for the train to start moving again so my father told Roger thank you, and we climbed down the metal ladder and went back to our seats in the passenger section. As I stared out the window I heard the train whistle blow two times, and the train began to move. I said to my father, "When I grow up I want to be an engineer, just like engineer Roger. I love trains, but there sure is a lot to learn."

My father squeezed my shoulder and said, "There sure is."

It took several days on the train to get all the way to Chicago. I began to think we would never get there, but on the fourth day of our trip I woke up and the sun was shining brightly. My father joyfully told me, "Come on Harry, it is time to get around. We will be in Chicago in about an hour."

I could hardly believe it, I had been riding four whole days and nights, and we were finally arriving in Chicago, my mother's home-town. As we entered the massive train station, everyone in our train car stood up and stared out the windows in horror. Although the transit area had not been destroyed, there were miles of piled debris and ashes, every direction you looked.

We saw complete blocks covered in destroyed buildings with pillars piled on top of rubble and half burned lumber laying off to one side. In the middle of all the carnage, you could see proud arches and steeples standing tall refusing to be a part of the wreckage. There were isolated chimneys and braces standing all alone in the center of an entire block of total destruction; upright pillars that did not give in to the merciless fire.

Off in the distance, we could see tall modern brick buildings that looked unscathed; they appeared to have been miraculously missed by the fire. I saw large buildings that looked totally intact, except as you looked closer you could see that every window had been blown out from all the floors of the structure. The building had survived, but it would need to be taken down because the structure was destroyed by the fire, and it was deemed condemned.

It had been months since the Great Chicago fire, but they had nowhere to put all of the burned ashes, debris and destroyed lumber so they stacked it in large piles. There was so much rubble that even after several months, much of the damaged city had not even been touched yet. The people were desperately working together, trying to get their city back to some sort of normalcy.

It eventually took years to clean everything up, and when the city started to rebuild the population exploded. The city was rebuilt in brick and mortar instead of lumber and boards. Economic development eventually occurred and architects created a modern city with the world's first skyscrapers, but on the day that we arrived, the city was still trying to clean up from the fire.

As we pulled into the station and stopped, many of the people in our train car began wailing and screaming, because they could not believe what they were seeing. They had not been to the city since the fire had taken place, and they were horrified. I was just a child, but I knew that I would never forget the images that I witnessed that day. I would never get over the shock and total ruin that I saw. The city of Chicago looked like a war zone.

My mother appeared to be traumatized as she glared out the window. There is no way that she could have ever been prepared for all of the devastation that she witnessed. She covered her face with both of her hands and wept as my father held her securely. Although, she had received letters telling of the destruction, she was not ready for the utter obliteration that she saw. She had been to this train station many times throughout her lifetime; but this time nothing around her was recognizable.

As we carefully got off of the train, we were met on the station platform by my Aunt Charlotte and her husband Phillip. Aunt Charlotte was my mother's older sister. She was the sister who had written my mother to tell her that their father was ill and in the hospital.

After hugs and kisses, they helped us with our luggage and placed everything in a white carriage and we immediately headed for the hospital where my grandfather was staying. As soon as we were on our way Aunt Charlotte told my mother, "We told Father four days ago that you would be arriving soon. He immediately began to improve. He has been eating again, and he has even been sitting up in bed since we told him you were coming." Charlotte smiled at me and said, "He can hardly wait to meet his new grandson, Harry."

Charlotte was beautiful like my mother. She was soft-spoken and smiled when she talked, and she squeezed my mother's hand and said, "I am so glad you came to Chicago, this has been a very difficult time, but I think you will make all of us feel better."

My mother clutched her sister's hand and said, "I hope so." My mother looked over towards me and whispered to Charlotte, "We have been so anxious for everyone to meet Harry." She spoke quieter, but I could still hear her as she said, "Oh Charlotte, Harry is so wonderful, Andrew and I feel so blessed. We know that God sent him to us, and he has brought such happiness to our home. He has made our world complete. We couldn't ask for a more perfect child. He is healthy, handsome and so intelligent." My mother gently dotted the tears from her eyes before saying, "It has been hard for us to stay away, I wanted to come right after the fire, but we were trying to give everyone a little time to clean up the city."

As we rode away from the train station, we traveled straight through the worst part of the demolition. Narrow pathways had been cleared so that carriages and wagons could get through for people to get around. We passed by horse-drawn wagons filled with rubble and large piles of debris. It was absolutely amazing because after driving through the chaos that had been left behind by the inferno, we came to the outskirts of the destroyed area, and it just changed. We left the burned region and came to the section of the city that had not been affected by the fire. The streets were clean and well maintained, and we could tell that this is where the fire had stopped.

The streets were lined in neatly organized boardwalks, with trees and flowers and wonderful stately buildings. This was the city of Chicago that my mother had marveled about. There were ladies in long flowing dresses carrying lacey parasols, and gentlemen in brown three-piece suits walking casually down the boardwalks in their shiny two-toned shoes. We saw shopkeepers sweeping off the sidewalks, and people smiling, and laughing as if they hadn't a care in the world.

We watched children licking ice cream cones, and groups of girls jumping rope. I saw a man selling newspapers and magazines, and one store displayed rows of brightly colored fresh fruits and vegetables. There were ladies in fine dresses, sitting in restaurants having tea. This was a city of contentment and wealth. It was a completely different world than the destroyed area that we first saw when we got to Chicago that morning.

After traveling through the city for several minutes, we arrived at a large building and Uncle Phillip pulled the carriage into the front area and one by one we all got out. He then took the carriage over in the shade to wait until we returned.

As we entered the hospital, Aunt Charlotte led us directly down a long dark hall to where my grandfather's room was located. The hospital was quiet and dismal, and it had no windows and very few light fixtures. The walls were painted a dirty green color, and the entire building had kind of an odd musty, medicine smell.

We passed by several nurses in white dresses with little pointed white hats on their heads. They each wore a kind of cape that lightly draped around their shoulders, and every nurse seemed stern and very fervent about their work. Only a few smiled or even looked up as we walked by. I had never seen a nurse before, but I sensed they were very serious about their work. Each nurse carried small trays filled with water, utensils and smelly medicines. As a young child, the whole place kind of frightened me.

When we came to the room of my grandfather, I shyly hid behind my father's leg. Only two visitors were allowed in the room at one time. So Aunt Charlotte went in first, followed closely by my mother.

My grandfather was sitting up in bed eating when they entered the room. I could hear the delight in my grandfather's voice as he saw my mother walk slowly towards his hospital bed.

I could hear them softly whispering as I stood outside the door. Suddenly, my Aunt Charlotte motioned for me to enter the room and meet my grandfather for the first time. Then she quietly slipped out so that I could take her place in the hospital room.

I thought to myself, "My grandfather; my very own Chicago grandfather. I have never had a Chicago grandfather before. I wondered what it will be like to have a Chicago grandfather, the father of my mother." I cautiously walked up next to my mother and stared at the older man sitting up in the bed. The man was pale with white hair, and he looked much thinner than any of the other men that I had met in my lifetime, but he smiled and I knew right away that he was glad that I had come to Chicago.

My mother reached down and lifted me up, so that I was the same height as my grandfather. My mother talked softly directly in my ear and said, "Harry, this is your grandfather, Richard W. Bates. He is my father, and a

United States Senator from Illinois." She kissed me on the cheek as she said, "Father this is my son, Harry, Harrison Andrew Langley."

My grandfather held out his right hand to shake my hand and he smiled as he said, "Nice to meet you Harrison Andrew Langley. I have waited a long time to meet my first and only grandson." I could tell that my grandfather was truly a gentleman. He smiled a huge smile at me when he told me, "You have three girl cousins, but you are the only grandson that your grandmother, Marjorie and I have. Your Aunt Charlotte has two daughters, Diane Elizabeth and Gwyneth, and your Uncle Douglas has Candace, but you are the only young man in our family." My grandfather kept smiling as he talked, but soon he had tears in his eyes as he whispered, "We have waited a long time for a grandson, and I am so glad you are finally here."

I knew right away that I liked having him for a grandfather. He made me feel happy inside, so I told him, "Thank you Grandfather, I'm glad I am here too."

For some reason that made my grandfather laugh, but my mother hugged me extra tight, so I knew it was a joyful kind of laugh. So, I laughed real loud too. It felt good to laugh with my grandfather. I loved having a family. The more my grandfather laughed, the more I laughed and the better my grandfather looked, after he started laughing he didn't seem as sickly as before.

After visiting for a few minutes, my mother put me down on a chair by the bed, and then left to have my father come in the room to see my grandfather. As my father entered the room, he walked over and picked me up and I told him, "Father this is my brand-new grandfather, Richard W. Bates." Again my father and my grandfather both laughed out loud, but I wasn't sure why. I was too young to realize that my father and my grandfather had known each other for many years, and that my grandfather was only brand-new to me.

My father grinned and squeezed me tight and leaned his forehead up to mine and said, "Oh Harry you are such a joy, and such young gentleman."

"Yes, yes he certainly is a polite gentleman," my grandfather stated. "And he truly is a blessed addition to our family."

As they were talking, a nurse walked into the room and said, "Senator, it is time for your medicine, and all of your visitors need to leave so that you can rest."

My grandfather grumbled, "Oh nonsense, I feel better than I have in weeks, and all I have done since I got here is rest."

"Now Senator Bates, you know what the doctor said. You need to rest," the nurse persisted without backing down an inch.

My father and I headed for the door and my father promised my grandfather, "Senator, you rest now and Harry and I will be back later to make sure you did as the doctor ordered." We both smiled and waved at my grandfather as my father carried me out of the room.

As we walked back down the dismal hallway to go find Uncle Phillip and the carriage, my Aunt Charlotte commented, "Father looks so much better than he did a few weeks ago. The doctors had given him little chance of recovery, but look at him now that your family is here. He is eating, talking, sitting up in bed, and he is even laughing. I haven't heard him laugh since the fire occurred." My mother and my Aunt Charlotte linked arm in arm as they happily walked out into the sunlight to get into the carriage.

After we were all in the carriage, Aunt Charlotte told us, "You will be staying with us in a big hotel just a few blocks from here. It is where our family has been living since the fire destroyed everything. It is a fairly nice hotel and many of the people staying there were our neighbors from the city."

Within minutes, Uncle Phillip parked the carriage up next to a large brick building, and we all got out to go see the place where we would be living for the next couple of months.

The apartment was large and brightly decorated. It had several bedrooms, one of which I would be sharing with my two cousins while we stayed in Chicago. As I shyly entered the apartment, I was met at the door by my grandmother Marjorie, and one of my cousins, Diane Elizabeth.

Diane Elizabeth was tall and thin with long curly blond ringlets that bounced as she walked. She was the older of the two girls, and to a four-year-old like me, she seemed really grown-up. She was ten years old and she appeared to be about the same age of Aunt Etta's twin girls, Carolyn and Constance.

She wore a neatly tailored light blue dress with ruffled sleeves and a kind of ruffled white apron in the front. She instantly got down on her knees in front of me and smiled and hugged me hello and said, "Oh Harry, I am so glad you are finally here. Gwyneth, Grandmother and I made fresh sugar cookies with bright sprinkles on them, just for you."

Before we could head for the kitchen to retrieve the cookies, Gwyneth came bouncing out of the bedroom with a large colored welcome sign that she had patiently been working on for our family's arrival. Gwyneth was seven years old and was just learning to write her letters. She also wore a neatly tailored dress, much like her sister's, only her dress was a light green color. She too had bouncy blonde curls and a big hair bow right in the center of her head. She looked just like her sister Diane Elizabeth, only younger.

Gwyneth quickly wrapped her arms tightly around my neck, and kissed my cheek before I had time to refuse. Then she said, "Oh Harry I am so glad you are here for a visit. We will have such fun while you and your family are in Chicago."

When she released her grasped from around my shoulders, I innocently smiled and nodded my head up and down hoping that she wouldn't grab me again. I said nothing as I stood back and stared. I had never been around such friendly, exuberant young girls before. I didn't even know them, but they acted as if they knew me.

71

Marilynn J. Harris

All of my brothers and sisters in Aunt Etta's family were not huggers or squeezers. I had only been hugged like that one time before, and that was by my sister Mary, on the last night that we were together. That night we held each other and cried on each other's shoulder after the men on the horses had visited our camp by the river. The next day I was sent away, and I never saw any of the family again. For one second my heart hurt as I reminisced about my other family. After all of this time, I still missed Aunt Etta, Titus and all of my brothers and sisters, and I probably always will.

Five days after we arrived in Chicago, my grandfather had improved so much that he was released from the hospital, and he was able to return home to the hotel where we all shared an apartment. It was a miracle how quickly my grandfather recuperated once our family arrived. He just got stronger every day, and soon he was up taking walks and watching all of us play games out in the front yard area.

I enjoyed sitting and visiting with my grandfather; he told me all about his job as a senator of Illinois, and of his time in the war. He had a beautiful solid gold pocket watch that played music every hour, and each time the music would begin, my grandfather would pull his watch out of his pocket and check to make sure that it was still keeping good time. He checked his watch every hour of the day, each time the music began to sound. Grandfather said that he checked it continually because it was an old antique watch that had been in his family for several generations. My grandfather told me, "It was given to my father by my grandfather, and my father handed it down to me."

He said, "It is a very expensive timepiece because it is solid gold with small diamonds scattered throughout the outside casing, and it is one of a kind. The first pocket watch was created in the mid-fifteenth century by a German locksmith. Those watches were called a Nuremburg watch or a pomander watch." My grandfather shook his head back and forth and said, "This watch was made a century later as a special gift for my grandfather, Governor John. W. Ainsworth. It was a unique trial creation developed as

72

a birthday gift just for him, but it proved to be too expensive to ever reproduce. It was the only one made." My grandfather smiled, "I am still amazed at how it continues to keep working year after year, just as it did when it was new. If its stops working, all you have to do is open it up, and set it in the sunlight, and it will start working once again. I don't think there was another watch made at that time that was even similar to this sunlight timepiece. "

My grandfather let me hold the pocket watch and I was surprised at how heavy it was. I chuckled every time the music began to play; because I knew within seconds my grandfather would pull the shiny gold watch out of his breast pocket, and check the time. He really liked that watch.

My family loved Chicago and I soon learned that we had a close-knit family that truly cared about each other. It didn't take me long before I sincerely appreciated the hugs and kisses from my cousins. It was completely different staying in Chicago than it was in Tennessee, but it was a good kind of different. Although, I missed my horse, River, and my friends from our church, I also treasured my time visiting with my relatives. Having family was wonderful. I loved getting together with my grandparents, and all of my aunts, uncles and cousins. I cherished having a place where I belonged.

Even in the short time that we were there in Chicago, we watched much of the destroyed area get cleaned up and readied for the town to rebuild. The last of the rubbish and ash was just pushed into the river so that the area could be cleared and usable. Once the construction begin the gutted area was rapidly replaced with steel beams and solid concrete structures. The city of Chicago vowed that it would never again be exposed to anything like they had been forced to endure with the fire.

The mayor stated at a town meeting, "The buildings of Chicago will be built bigger, taller, sturdier and indestructible. From this day forward the city of Chicago will have buildings so tall that they reach the clouds. People from all over the world will flock to live in our great city." He went on,

"We will one day be the most populous city of the United States." The crowds cheered at his uplifting optimism for the future of their great city.

The transformation after the fire was exciting to watch. A large portion of the city had been destroyed by the terrible fire, but the people were determined. Everyone worked together and they were unwavering, they pushed forward and they would survive; soon the city of Chicago would be completely reestablished.

My grandfather finally went back to work, it was incredible; his health was almost completely restored. Within months all of my relatives would be able to move back into their newly renovated neighborhoods. Although we were excited for them, my parents and I realized that it would soon be time to go back to our own home. Our time in Chicago was over, and I felt saddened when my parents told me it was time for us to return home to Tennessee. We had stayed much longer than we had originally planned.

My cousins hovered near the bed, as I slowly helped my mother pack my suitcase with my neatly cleaned clothes to take back with me on the train. I had grown extremely close to my cousins Diane Elizabeth and Gwyneth. I had gotten used to their loving hugs, and all of the hand-holding as they led me around the sidewalks and parks as we took long walks. I knew that I would miss them more than words could ever express. They helped fill a huge whole in my heart that had been left there after the loss of Aunt Etta, Titus and my brothers and sisters. I discovered that cousins were a special kind of family. They held a unique place in my life; a place that no one else on earth could ever fill.

I had my other cousin Candace, but she was really quiet, and reserved. Although, we were only a few years apart she seemed much older, and she lived on the other end of town with her parents Douglas and Holly, and we rarely saw her. She was tall and slender with long dark hair, and deep green eyes. Candace was a ballerina and she spent several hours each day practicing her ballet. I could hardly talk when she came around, because she was so beautiful. She was a hugger too, but not so much to me. She mainly hugged Diane Elizabeth and Gwyneth.

As we stood in front of the hotel that we had been sharing with the family for the past few months, each person gave long hugs and kisses, before our family climbed up into the carriage. I held back tears as I waved goodbye to all of my aunts, uncles, cousins and my grandparents. Our family was saddened to have to leave and return back to Tennessee, but we had been in Chicago for many months, and it was time to go home.

I stood up in the carriage and watched behind us, and I continued to wave all of the way down the street until I could no longer see my precious cousins; my new best friends Diane Elizabeth and Gwyneth. My heart wanted to cry out when I could no longer see them, but instead I sat down in the seat to continue on with my parents to the train station.

We traveled back through the city the exact way that we had traveled when we had first arrived, but the city of Chicago looked much different now. The streets were cleaned and swept, and all of the debris and clutter was gone. We could tell that the mayor was right, the city of Chicago would soon be great again.

Taking the train back to Tennessee would be different for me than when we had first come. I was no longer surprised to see the steam streaming out from the sides of the engines, and I was no longer scared to climb the platform and walk into the passenger car. Instead, I now was a seasoned rider, and I haughtily said hello to every person on the train as I escorted my parents down the aisle to find our seats.

I was cheerful and proud, and excited to begin the new adventure of riding over high trestles and crossing long bridges again. I looked forward to seeing the fields filled with horses, cows and daisies. I anxiously awaited the many new faces as the train stopped at each train station and let some passengers off while other people got on.

Marilynn J. Harris

Soon the train whistled blew twice, and the train began to move. We were told that it would take a day longer to get back home because the train was forced to reroute through Iowa because they were replacing the wooden tracks between Chicago and St. Louis, Missouri. Although the entire train system was fairly new, we remembered that engineer Roger had told us that many of the tracks were improperly made to begin with.

They were now forced to do the tracks over to make them stronger so that the trains can travel faster and smoother. It didn't matter to me, I loved traveling on the train, and I was excited to see a new area.

On the second day as we were traveling near Adair, Iowa, I heard the train whistle blow several short pulls in a row. I instantly looked at my father, because I knew that was a signal for danger. Before anyone had time to question the situation, the brakes locked on, and the train instantly slowed down.

As we stared out the window, we saw three men on horseback, they were shooting bullets in the air, and shouting at the engineer to come to a complete stop. The men had stopped the train and were robbing the express safe. I sat helplessly in my seat as I watched in horror as the three robbers dressed in white Ku Klux Klan hoods stole the money out of the baggage car, and rode off with the cash box.

The robbers never entered the passenger cars, and they didn't harm one person on the train. They were only there for the cash in the safe, apparently they knew exactly where it was, and how much money the train would be carrying.

After they were completely out of sight, I buried my head under my mother's arm and continued to quiver; I was afraid to look up. My mother held me close to her for several minutes, because she knew that this was not the first time that I had seen the men on horseback, wearing the terrifying Ku Klux Klan outfits.

My brother Nicolas had told her of the chilling encounter that the black families in our group had witnessed the night before I arrived at the big white house. Although, these riders seemed somehow different than the men that I saw that first night, fear still crept over me.

After a few minutes, I fell asleep cuddled up against my mother's arm. When I woke up, the train was once again moving. I could hear everyone around me talking and I discovered that one of the robbers was Jesse James the notorious bank robber, and the other two men were part of his gang. They had stolen $3,000 in cash from the train's safe.

Jesse James was an American outlaw, bank robber and train robber. He was from St. Joseph, Missouri, and he was the most famous member of the James-Younger gang. Jesse and his brother Frank were Bushwhackers and they were accused of committing atrocities against the Union soldiers.

One man on the train that actually knew the James family said, "Jesse James came from a good family. His father Robert S. James was a commercial hemp farmer and a Baptist minister. He was very prosperous and owned more than 100 acres of farmland in Bradford, Missouri. Before Jesse was born Robert James had helped found the William Jewell College in Liberty, Missouri. He died during the Gold Rush days while he was being a minister to the men searching for gold." The man sadly said, "Jesse was only three years old when his father died."

I knew that the name Jesse James would be someone that I would always remember. Throughout my lifetime he was often talked about not only as a bank robber and train robber, but as a legendary Robin Hood. Of course, I would remember him because he was famous, but also, because I had personally seen him that day, when I was four years old, and he robbed the Rock Island Express as we traveled home from Chicago, through Adair, Iowa.

His gang robbed many banks, but for some reason he seemed to be well-liked and respected. Even before I was born, he had organized the first daylight bank robbery in United States history. The robbery was on

Marilynn J. Harris

Valentine's Day in 1866 and they made off with $57,000 in cash of the citizens of Liberty, Missouri.

The James-Younger gang was most active from 1866 until 1876 around that time several of his gang members were killed during a bank robbery in Northfield, Minnesota. They recruited new members, but they were all being chased by the law. Jesse and his brother Frank moved to Nashville, Tennessee and changed their names to Thomas Howard and B.J. Woodson. On April 3, 1882, Jesse James was killed by Robert Ford, one of his own gang members. Ford shot unarmed Jesse James in the back of the head, just to collect the reward money.

Seven

Yellow Fever

About six months after we got home from our trip to Chicago, my grandparents that lived in Memphis came to live with us. They were my father's parents, Andrew Thomas Langley Sr., and my grandmother, Henrietta Langley. Like thousands of other people that lived in the city, they left to escape the deadly epidemic, Yellow Fever.

They just boarded up their beautiful brick home and moved in with us. They stayed with us for several years because they were afraid to move back to Memphis. We had plenty of room, and I loved having my grandparents there. Yellow Fever never effected anyone on our plantation, but by the year 1873 approximately 2,000 people in Memphis had died of the highly contagious epidemic and more than 25,000 people had left the city.

By the time the epidemic was controlled, a total of around 17,000 people had actually come down with Yellow Fever and approximately 5,150 of them had died. It was eventually discovered that the fatal disease was caused by mosquitoes.

People lived in fear of returning to the city long after the epidemic had passed, so our grandparents remained on the plantation with us, just to be safe. In 1879 so many people had died from Yellow Fever or had left the city that Memphis lost its charter and went bankrupt.

A freed black man by the name of Robert R. Church Sr. came forward to help out the desperate city. He became known as the south's first African-American millionaire. He bought a bond for $1,000 to pay off the debt and help restore the city charter. He became wealthy by buying property after the people left. He founded the first black owned bank, Solvent Savings Bank in Memphis. He made improvements in the sanitation, sewer and removed the mosquito breeding grounds.

I felt sorry for the people of Memphis, but I loved the time that my grandparents stayed with us. I was almost five years old when they first arrived at the plantation and they lived with us for most of my early years. My grandfather taught me how to play chess, and my grandmother taught me how to read and to write before I ever started school.

I never wanted them to move back to the city, I wanted them to live with us forever. I cherished having a family, because I was their only grandchild and they treated me like a prince.

Shortly after my grandparents moved in with us, President Grant established the world's first national park. It was called Yellowstone National Park. It was a huge park covering many parts of Wyoming, Montana and Idaho. The first day that I heard about the park, I sat down on the floor and carefully studied the glorious pictures that were on the front page of the newspaper. The new park had green pools, large meadows and tall geysers of billowing steam. I was fascinated by all of the pictures. I had never seen any place like it before.

I saved the newspaper pictures under my bed, and every day I would pull the newspaper out and look at it. My grandfather watched me stare at the pictures day after day. I would quietly lie on my belly, out on the front porch, and study the pictures until the newspaper grew wrinkled and tattered and hard to read. I was completely engrossed by the unusual snapshots.

As a special surprise for my fifth birthday, my grandfather ordered me a group of unique photographs that were taken throughout the park. The park had only been in existence less than six months, and it was still too rustic for visitors, but I loved the beautiful photographs that Grandpa had purchased for me. Yellowstone National Park was unlike any other park in the world.

Throughout the years that my grandparents stayed with us, we took many extended vacations. They seemed to enjoy sharing their excursions with us, and I liked seeing new places. Sometimes we would travel by ship and go and see other countries. Oftentimes my father would not travel with us, but my mother never let me go without her. She was always there to share my excitement.

In 1876 our family went to the Centennial International Exhibition. It was the first official World's Fair in the United States that was held in Philadelphia, Pennsylvania, from May to November. The fair was celebrating the 100th anniversary of the signing of the Declaration of Independence in Philadelphia. It was held in Fairmont Park along the Schuylkill River on the fairgrounds designed by Herman J. Schwartzman. Nearly ten million visitors attended the exhibition.

The Centennial Exhibition showcased mass-products such as sewing machines and typewriters. It was the first great gathering of machine tool building and assembly equipment vendors in the United States. There were thousands of exhibits and products on display. It featured more than 30,000 exhibitors in 190 buildings on a 256 acre site.

Marilynn J. Harris

One of the highlights of the fair was the first public showing of the arm and torch of the statue of liberty (the rest of the giant structure would not be complete in New York Harbor until 1886.)

The Centennial Expedition also witnessed the world's first monorail system with a steam locomotive and a passenger car. It had a single elevated iron rail above the ground.

A 29 years old inventor by the name of Alexander Graham Bell, shared his newly patented invention, called the prototype telephone. Bell invented a device that combined the 'harmonic telegraph' with the aspects of the telegraph and the record player to allow individuals to speak to each other from a distance.

Alexander Graham Bell was a teacher at the Pemberton Avenue School for the deaf in Boston, Massachusetts. (Bell eventually married one of his students from his class.)

Also, the phonograph and the first incandescent light bulb was invented in Menlo Park by Thomas Edison. Edison once said, "We will make electricity so cheap, that only the rich will burn candles." Thomas Edison also displayed "the automatic telegraph system."

One of the most impressive buildings that we saw was the 558,000 square foot Machinery Hall. It was a giant glass and iron structure that was filled with hand tools, machine tools, pulleys and miles of overhead belts. There were over 8,000 operating machines in the 14 acre building.

There was a steam engine so large that it powered the entire exhibition and proved to the 34 nations and 20 colonies who exhibited at the fair that not only was the USA an equal with European nations in manufactured goods, but had surpassed them in innovation.

Another product that made its debut was a mineral that was discovered in Quebec, Canada called asbestos. People marveled at the revolutionary new material because of its fire-proof quality.

The Centennial International Exhibition was an exciting time of transformation for the United States of America. We witnessed so many wonderful life-changing innovations at the fair. My family knew that our lives would forever be improved because of the thousands of new inventions that were displayed at the exhibition. 1876 was a major time of change in America's history and we had witnessed many of the changes first hand.

****

A few months after we returned from the fair, my grandmother received a disturbing letter about her cousin. On June 25, 1876 the Battle of Little Big Horn occurred in the eastern Montana territory. The battle is commonly referred to as "Custer's last stand." The battle took place between the Cavalry and the northern tribe Indians, including the Cheyenne, Sioux and the Arapaho. It was between the 7th Cavalry Regiment of the United States Army and the tribes. The battle occurred near the Little Big Horn River.

The most prominent actions of the Great Sioux War of 1876 was five of the 7th Cavalry's twelve companies were annihilated. Custer was killed as were two of his brothers. The total U.S. causality count included 268 dead and 55 severely wounded including four Crow Indian scouts and two Pawnee Indian scouts.

My grandmother's cousin was killed in that battle. He was one of the commanding officers in the 7th Cavalry Regiment. She had not seen her cousin for many years, but she reminisced of the skinny, freckled-faced boy of her youth. She said her cousin, Clarence had never married. He left home at seventeen to join the army and never returned.

****

Marilynn J. Harris

Shortly after my twelfth birthday, my grandparents decided to move back home to Memphis. Although we all loved living on the plantation together, my grandparents felt it was time for them to go back to the city. They still owned their house, and it had been boarded up and empty for almost seven years. They received word that the people of Memphis were slowly returning to the abandoned city, and it was time for them to go home too.

My grandparents were shocked when they returned and discovered how many people had died during the Yellow Fever epidemic. Almost every family in the city had been somehow affected. They had lost many of their neighbors and over half of the people in their church had left the city and never returned.

When my grandparents moved back to Memphis after all of those years, it was like they were moving to a brand new city, and in many ways it was a new city. There were lots of changes taking place, and by the 20th century Memphis, Tennessee, was the largest cotton market and hardwood lumber market in the world.

Eight

The Brooklynn Bridge

In May of 1883, my father planned an amazing family business trip for all of us to New York City. The Brooklynn Bridge was to be unveiled on the 24th of May and my parents and my grandparents from Chicago planned to be there for the huge event. The long train trip from Memphis to New York was 1,096 miles, but my parents new this would be an adventure of a lifetime for me. I had just turned 16 years old and I could hardly wait to go to see New York City for the first time. My dad traveled to New York at least once a year, but of course my mother and I never went with him.

By the year 1883, the country had seen an increase in over 73, 000 new miles of railroad built. Roughly, over 7,000 miles each year with much of that being built in the south and western areas of the nation. The trains traveled so much faster in 1883 than they did when we took our first trip to Chicago when I was four years old. The trains could now travel up to 80 miles an hour and they were a much smoother ride.

The Brooklynn Bridge was a hybrid cable-stayed/suspension bridge that connects the borough of Manhattan and Brooklynn by spanning the East River. When the bridge was completed, it was 1,595.5 feet long and it was the first steel wire suspension bridge ever constructed. The bridge was originally referred to as the New York and Brooklynn Bridge and also the East River Bridge.

My family arrived in New York on May 19th; five days before the big Brooklynn Bridge event was to take place. We met my grandparents, Richard and Marjorie Bates and their best friends, William and Loretta Spencer at the Hotel Chelsea around 2:00 in the afternoon. My grandparents had brought my eighteen-year-old cousin Gwyneth with them, and the Spencer's brought their fifteen year old granddaughter, Margaret Ruth.

My cousin Gwyneth and I had remained close throughout the years, ever since we first met when I was only four years old. She had been one of my best friends most of my life, in fact since I was an only child, she was more like a sister to me than a cousin.

My mother and I went to Chicago to visit our family at least once a year, and each time we went it was like none of the cousins had ever been apart. Gwyneth and her sister Diane Elizabeth had even come to Tennessee on two different holidays, and last summer we went to Chicago for Diane's wedding.

The unveiling of the Brooklynn Bridge would be a life-changing event for all of us and the grandparents didn't want any of the grandchildren to miss out. The three of us, Gwyneth, Margaret Ruth and I were the youngest children from each family, so we were lucky to be able to come to the grand presentation of the new bridge.

The unveiling of the bridge was phenomenal. There were thousands of people there to experience the opening of the giant bridge. The bridge had taken over 14 years to construct. Six hundred workers had worked on the bridge, at a cost of fifteen million dollars. At least two dozen people had died during the construction of the bridge, including the original bridge designer himself, John Roebling

John Augustus Roebling was born in Germany in 1806, he graduated from the Royal Polytechnics Institution in Berlin. At the age of 25 years old, he immigrated to the United States to pursue a career in engineering. His plans changed, and he moved to western Pennsylvania where he decided to try farming. After five years, he got married and had a son and moved to Harrisburg to be a civil engineer. There he created a wire rope factory.

He earned a reputation as an advisor of suspension bridges, but many of the bridges failed under strong winds and heavy loads. Roebling created the technology of a web truss that stabilized the bridge of Niagara Gorge at Niagara Falls, New York, and the Ohio River in Cincinnati.

That is why the New York legislators approved Roebling's plan for a suspension bridge over the East River between Manhattan and Brooklynn. It would be the longest steel suspension bridge in the world. It would be 1,600 feet from tower to tower.

When construction began in 1869, John Roebling was fatally injured while he was standing at the edge of the dock, deciding the exact location where the bridge would be built. His foot was crushed by an arriving ferry. His injured toes were amputated, but he refused further medical treatment, and he felt he could heal his foot by cleaning it regularly with water. His condition deteriorated. John Roebling died 24 days later of tetanus. He died on July 22, 1869 and his 32 year old son, Washington A. Roebling took over the building of the bridge. Washington Roebling had worked with his father on several bridges, and had helped design the Brooklynn Bridge with him since its beginning.

Marilynn J. Harris

The workers on the bridge had to excavate the riverbed in massive wood boxes called caissons. These airtight chambers were pinned to the river's floor by enormous granite blocks. Pressurized air was pumped into the chambers to keep water and debris out.

The workers were known as sandhogs, many of them were immigrants earning only about $2.00 a day. The sandhogs used shovels and dynamite to clear away the mud and boulders on the bottom of the river.

When they reached 44 feet on the Brooklynn side and 78 feet on the Manhattan side, they put down granite, then worked their way back up to the surface. The journey to and from the depths of the East River could be deadly. To get to the caissons, they rode in small iron containers called airlocks. As the men worked in the caissons, they were hot and they developed blinding headaches, itchy skin, bloody noses and slowed heartbeats.

Many developed caisson's disease, or the bends. The effects were joint pain, paralysis, convulsions, numbness, speech impediments and sometimes even death. More than 100 people suffered from the disease, including Washington Roebling himself who remained partially paralyzed for the rest of his life after developing the condition. He was forced to watch the remainder of the building of the bridge with a telescope and his wife, Emily took charge of the bridge project.

Several other people also died from accidents, collapses, fires and explosions during the construction of the bridge. The bridge was finally ready to be unveiled on May 24, 1883, and thousands of people were there for the ceremonies, including my family and friends.

The dedication ceremony was delivered by President Chester A. Arthur and the New York Governor, Grover Cleveland. Emily Roebling was the first person to travel over the completed bridge. She crossed the bridge with a rooster sitting on her lap, as a symbol of victory.

Within 24 hours, an estimated 250,000 people walked across the bridge using the roadway that John A. Roebling had designed. My parents, my grandparents, the Spencers, their granddaughter Margaret Ruth, my cousin Gwyneth and I were among the 250,000 people who crossed the bridge that day.

It was breath-taking to be one of the first people to ever cross the enormous structure. The bridge span was 1600 feet across from tower to tower, it was 85 feet wide and 270 feet high. Being one of the first people amongst the masses to cross the new bridge, was an experience that none of us would ever forget, no matter how many other times we would cross the bridge throughout our lifetime.

For several years after it was unveiled, it remained the tallest structure in the western hemisphere. It was soon dubbed the eighth wonder of the world, and in 1898 the city of Brooklynn formerly merged with New York City.

After the bridge dedication, our families stayed in New York for several more days. While we were there, we went to the ballet to watch my beautiful cousin Candace in the production of Swan Lake. Although the production of Swan Lake did not review well, I thought my cousin's performance was magnificent, and she grew more striking every time I saw her. She had enchanted me since I was a small child, although she never knew it.

Her skin was like porcelain, and her thick dark hair was perfectly groomed; but it was her eyes, her deep sparkling green eyes that kept me completely captivated. She was so slender and graceful and I had to catch my breath each time she glanced my way. Although I was only sixteen years old and she was two years older than me, I thought she was the most beautiful woman that was ever born. I sometimes fantasized that when we grew up Candace would finally notice me, and we would fall in love and get married. After all, she wasn't my real cousin.

Marilynn J. Harris

I loved being in New York. Gwyneth, Margaret Ruth, and I had so much fun together. It was great having the girls there to hang out with. New York was so totally different for me after being raised in Tennessee on the plantation. Gwyneth had visited New York several times before, so she was not only the oldest of the three of us, but she was the most familiar.

Our families had been together in New York for over a week, and as the three of us sat across the dinner table laughing and whispering secrets to each other, I finally noticed how pretty Margaret Ruth was. She had long, thick blond hair, and blue eyes with thick dark-black eye lashes. She was very quiet and reserved, not silly and outgoing like my cousin Gwyneth. I also noticed Margaret Ruth often just sat and listened, and studied me from across the table without joining in on the conversations.

She was petite and poised with soft feminine hands and long delicate fingers. She laughed when I laughed, and told me I was clever. With so much going on while we were in New York, I hadn't really even noticed her until it was almost time for us to leave. As we talked, I learned that her birthday was in May, and she was just a year younger than me. The more we talked the more I liked her.

On our last day in New York as we were preparing to go to the train, we all hugged each other goodbye. When it was time for me to hug Margaret Ruth goodbye, she shyly leaned up and kissed me on the cheek. I couldn't believe it, I had never been kissed by a girl before; at least not a beautiful girl, not a girl almost my age. I was feeling pretty good about myself as I got on the train and waved goodbye to the rest of the people in our group. We were the first train to leave the station, so I sat back in the train seat and smiled for several minutes, and just stared out the window.

Finally my mom broke the silence when she said, "Harry, that Margaret Ruth sure is a pretty young girl, isn't she?" My mom grinned at me and said, "And she sure seems to like you."

I didn't realize until then that my dad was also smiling at me. My father spoke up and said, "The Spencer's are really nice people, and their granddaughter seems like a nice young lady as well."

I couldn't help it, I smiled as I shook my head up and down and said, "Yes, yes she seems like a really nice girl, and she is rather pretty." I continued, "I promised I would come visit her next time we are in Chicago."

Both my parents slowly nodded their heads up and down at the same time, and smugly looked at each other and smiled.

****

As I had promised, I visited Margaret Ruth several different times in Chicago when I would go to see my grandparents and my cousins. In fact, we saw each other two or three times a year for the next several years. We went to dinner parties, the theatre, community balls, and had family picnics in the park. She was so easy to be around and the more we talked the more comfortable we were together. Our families had been friends for years, and they socialized together on a regular basis. Being with Margaret Ruth was very comfortable and natural.

After graduation from High School, I went away to Yale University to study law. Yale was one of the best law schools in the country. During my second semester, my mother sent me a telegram to inform me that my beloved horse, River had died during the night, and they had found him early that morning. I knew he was getting older, but the news still broke my heart. I had several other horses in my lifetime, but River was the pony of my youth. He had gotten me through so many tough times in my life.

I sat quietly on the side of my bed and wept for the loss of my dearest friend. Oftentimes, as I was growing up, I would go out to the barn, and sit in his stall for hours at a time, and share my deepest thoughts with him. I was an only child, and he was the closest thing I had to a brother. Although my life was almost perfect, I had so many questions about where I had come from. My parents had adopted me at three years old, but where I had actually been born was a mystery even to them.

My father and mother had always been completely honest about how God had sent me riding up on a mule one day, but I still had hundreds of unanswered questions as to who I really was. That is why I spent so much of my time talking to River about things.

I hadn't actually ridden him in years because he was such a small horse. I had gotten him when I was a child, and as an adult I have grown well over 6 feet tall, but he had been there for me all of life, almost as long as I had known my parents. I had just talked to him last month when I was home for the holidays. I often talked to River about things that I could not discuss with anyone else.

"I will miss him so much," I confessed to myself. I buried my face into my hands and whispered, "Run through the Heavens my cherished friend."

My time away at college was a very lonely time, and my cousin Candace often performed in New York while I was going to school at Yale. Many times I would ride the train and quietly go alone to the ballet and watch her perform as I sat high up in the balcony. I never told anyone about my secret adoration for Candace, but I thought she was absolutely wonderful. When I went to the ballet and secretly watched her, I didn't feel so alone. Being close to her made me feel like I was near family, even if we never spoke to each other.

I would sit somewhere out of sight, and proudly watch her perform. She was so graceful, elegant and poised. She was the epitome of perfection and beauty.

I had been so intimidated by her all of my life that I never talked when she was around, but I wanted to. I was so proud to be related to her. I always clapped loader than everyone else after each performance.

About twice a year, I would take the train from New York to Chicago to go and see Margaret Ruth and her family, and that also helped me with the loneliness. I had been visiting her for so many years that I felt like her grandparents were my grandparents, and they treated me like I was part of the family. We would all go and see plays, or to the opera, or attend fancy dinner parties together. The four of us enjoyed the same things, and I enjoyed going places with them.

Margaret Ruth was a very gentle person, yet intelligent and extremely confident. She was incredibly striking and lady-like, and even in her fancy high heeled shoes she was at least a head shorter than I was. Margaret Ruth was the perfect match for me. As we walked down the street arm in arm, she made me feel tall and strong like she needed me to protect her from the world. She brought out a kind of contentment in me that no one else ever did.

From the beginning of our relationship, the family knew that we would someday become man and wife. It was just expected, but because we were so young when we first met, waiting to get married until after college was never an issue.

In my second year of college, my mother received a letter announcing the wedding of my cousin Candace to her producer John H. Maxim. When I was told the news, I instantly felt ill. I knew that I had always had a secret infatuation for Candace, but I never realized until I got word that she was getting married that I may have actually loved her. The news of her marriage hit me hard.

"That is absurd," I thought to myself. "She is 'almost' my cousin, and besides I will one day marry Margaret Ruth like everyone expects me to do. Our marriage has been planned for years." Yet, my heart was quietly aching for the confusing love that could never be. I had idolized Candace ever since I was a child, and she had never done anything to make me think less of her, or to destroy my adoration. She was truly my first love, and I knew I would never love anyone the exact same way that I cared for her.

Nine

After All These Years

After graduating from law school, my parents helped me set up a law office in downtown Memphis. I planned to get the law office going before I settled down and married Margaret Ruth. I created the law office with one of the guys that I had graduated with, Jonathon Roark.

We found a perfect office space and we called the firm Langley & Roark. Jonathon and I had roomed together in college and we knew many of our ambitions and ideals were much the same. We got along really well. We were both engaged to be married, we both attended church, and we were only a few months apart in age.

Jonathon had come from a well-to-do family very similar to my family. Our main objective was to help people who needed help, but did not have a lot of money to hire a lawyer.

We had just opened our doors, when we received our first client, a young black boy by the name of Jeremiah. Jeremiah was around ten years old, and he just burst into our office right off of the street. He was really upset as he told me, "My sister is in the store two doors down, and the owner of the store is yelling at her and telling her she broke a glass jar." Jeremiah rapidly repeated, "My little sister didn't do nothing, I was there, I seen her, my sister didn't do nothing!" Jeremiah begged, "Please help her Mister, the store owner is hollering at her, and I'm afraid he will send her to jail."

I instantly grabbed my jacket and darted out the door following young Jeremiah down the street. Jonathan grabbed his jacket and followed close behind.

As we walked in the front door of the store, Jeremiah ran over to his sister where she was hysterically wailing as the store owner held her by the arm, and wouldn't let her go. She looked so small and fragile, and she appeared absolutely terrified.

Brave little Jeremiah started hitting at the store owner saying, "Leave my little sister alone, leave my sister be. She didn't do nothing to your old jar."

When the store owner looked up and saw Jonathon and me approaching, he instantly released the tearful girl, and changed his entire demeanor. He smiled a courteous smile, and acted as if he wasn't the least bit worried about the two black children any longer. He said to us, "Well, good afternoon gentlemen, what can I help you with?" He kept on talking as if we were there to shop, and he was no longer concerned about the broken jar.

I spoke up first and said, "I'm sorry, I understand this young lady accidently broke a glass jar of yours." I remained professional as I took my money pouch out of my pocket and insisted I pay for the broken jar that was destroyed. I looked directly at the store owner and stated, "I'm sorry, but my friend Jeremiah didn't tell me how much the broken jar cost. Of course I will be glad to pay for your loss." The store owner turned pale as he looked me in the face, but said nothing. "Does a silver dime cover it?" I politely said as I handed him the bright shiny dime.

"Yes, yes, that is more than enough," the nervous store owner whispered as he timidly reached for the dime. Then he uttered, "You say these children are friends of yours?"

I smiled as I firmly spoke, "Oh yes, they are two very nice young children, don't you agree?"

The store owner slowly shook his head up and down, then he turned around and grabbed a candy jar off of the counter and he rapidly said, "Maybe your two small friends would like a candy stick?" he said reaching down and handing each child a colored stick.

Both children looked first at me, and then at the store owner before politely telling the man thank you for the candy. Jonathon and I, and Jeremiah and his sister shook hands with the store owner, and said our goodbyes. I smiled at the store owner as I glanced around and told him, "You have a very nice store here. We will be back again to do business."

"Oh thank you, thank you," the store owner repeated as he walked the four of us to the front door so we could return to the office.

As we silently walked in the office and sat down, Jonathon smiled at me and said, "Did we win or lose our first case?"

I shook my head back and forth and chuckled, "I say we won, how about you?"

As we sat quietly in our office for the rest of the afternoon, we wondered who would be our next client. We both wanted to help people that needed help, but so far, after our first client, we were one silver dime in the hole.

****

The next morning as we arrived at the office to open for business, we noticed a pretty young black woman sitting on a bench waiting for us to arrive. As we walked up and unlocked the door, the woman stood up to get our attention. She held out her hand and proudly introduced herself as she stated, "Good morning gentleman my name is Mary Jordon, and I am the mother of Jeramiah and Elliana, the two children that you helped at the store yesterday,"

I smiled at her and said, "Oh yes, they seem like very nice children." I continued, "My name is Harry Langley and this is my partner Jonathon Roark, and about yesterday, we were just glad to be able to help."

She smiled a beautiful sincere smile at me and said, "I just came to tell you thank you for what you did for my children. They couldn't stop talking about how smart you are, and how you even encouraged the store owner to give them each a piece of candy." She shook her head back and forth and then covered her face with one hand before going on, "He has falsely accused my kids of breaking things several different times. I am surprised they even went back into that store again, because he has been so mean to them."

As I watched Mrs. Jordon talk, I realized that she reminded me of someone that I had met before, but I couldn't tell just who it was. I knew very few people that lived in Memphis, so I couldn't figure out where I would have seen her before. Yet, I was absolutely fascinated to listen to her talk, because she seemed so familiar. I could tell she was a very proud mother, a mother that truly loved her kids.

As we continued to talk, the mailman stepped in the door with the mail and said, "Morning Harrison, Jonathon, here's your mail" and the mailman quickly slipped right back out the door.

"Harrison?" Mrs. Jordon exclaimed, "Your name is Harrison? I knew I recognized those dark blue eyes, but you had blond curls the last time I saw you." Mrs. Jordon squealed as she stood up, "Harrison...Obadiah...Pike? I am Mary. Do you remember me?" Mrs. Jordon said with tears streaming down her cheeks as she whispered, "I am the daughter of Etta and Titus Lewis. I used to be your sister."

"Oh, no I'm sorry Mrs. Jordon you are mistaken," Jonathon interjected as he jumped out of his chair, "This man is Harrison Langley, and his parents are Andrew and Elizabeth Langley. Their plantation is about twenty-five miles out of Memphis."

Mrs. Jordon slightly glanced at Jonathon before looking back at me as she replied, "I know, I was born there."

I just sat in my chair and stared at Mary Jordon. I tried to move, I tried to talk, but my mind was whirling in circles. No wonder I recognized this woman, but I still couldn't move. I just sat and stared at my beautiful big sister, Mary. Finally, within a few seconds I came to my senses and I stood up and darted around the desk and held my wonderful sister in my arms. "My sister, my sister, my sister Mary," I kept repeating out loud. Talking louder and louder each time I said her name."

Jonathon just stood there confused with his mouth drooped wide open. "Your sister? He mouthed, "You have a black sister?"

"Oh Harrison, I have missed you so much," my sister said through her streaming tears. "After Nicolas took you away, we all cried for days. Nicolas took it the hardest though, because he was the one that had to take you to the plantation. Our family prayed for you every single night, in fact you are also in my children's prayers." She grinned as she told me, "Jeramiah and Elliana pray for you every night, and they've never even known who you were."

Mary told me, "I actually have four children, Robert Titus, Rebecca, and of course Jerimiah and Elliana. I am married to a minister named Harvey Jordon. We live on a small acreage about a mile out of Memphis." She smiled, "I have a large garden and we have chickens, goats and two cows." She bragged, "I make a pretty amazing pot of chicken and dumplings, and I would love to have you and your partner over to the house for dinner. I bet I could even cook up one of my famous apple pies, if you'd come."

I loved my sister Mary, even though I had not seen her for over twenty years. I told her, "Of course we will come," I answered looking over towards Jonathon as he agreeably nodded his head up and down.

I continued to share a few of the things that were going on in my life as I said, "I am engaged to beautiful lady from Chicago, named Margaret Ruth, and I am currently living with my grandparents, right here in Memphis, until I get married."

As Mary stood up to leave, she hugged me one last time and said, "I will send one of the kids down with a note to let you know when to come for dinner."

After she left, I looked over at Jonathon who was now sitting behind his desk looking completely confused, and I grinned at him and said, "It's a long story."

Over the next few weeks, our office became the talk of the town. We had clients from everywhere coming in for legal advice. Many people were members of Harvey Jordon's church. Apparently his church was a large church and the Jordons were very well-respected around town. Mary was delighted to tell everyone she talked to how proud she was to call me her "brother."

Ten

Margaret Ruth's Family

Two weeks after my sister Mary had been to my office, I received an instant telegram from my fiancé, Margaret Ruth. She begged me to take the train and meet her and her grandmother in St. Louis, Missouri and then we would all travel together to Oklahoma. She said they had received word that her mother was dying and they did not want to go see her alone. Margaret Ruth's grandfather was away on a business trip, and he was not available to travel with them. That is why they wanted me to go.

In all the years that I had known Margaret Ruth, they had never talked about her family, so I didn't even know that her parents were still alive. This all came as a shock to me, but I was more than happy to accompany the ladies on their trip.

Their train from Chicago would arrive in St. Louis at 10:35 a.m. the next morning. I could then transfer to their train, from my Memphis train, and travel on with them to Oklahoma. I felt sorry to hear about Margaret Ruth's mother, but I looked forward to finally meeting the family that she never talked about. I only knew her grandparents, and I loved them, so I was quite sure that I would also love her parents.

At 10:35 the next morning we made the connection, and we were all on our way to Oklahoma to see my future in-laws. I had never been to Oklahoma before, so I was anxious to see the area.

At dinner time, the three of us went into the dining car to have some dinner. I noticed that Grandmother Spencer was unusually quiet, and she looked pale and distraught. She seemed very withdrawn. I could tell that taking Margaret Ruth back to see her family after all of these years, was really upsetting her. Grandmother Spencer barely ate anything, she just picked at her food. As we sat around the table, Grandmother Spencer quietly asked me," How is your new law practice coming along. Have you had many clients yet?"

I scooted up closer to the table because I was excited to share my news of my sister Mary. I said, "I had the oddest thing happened on my second day of work…" I continued to share my story of the two children at the store. "But, the strangest thing yet, actually happened on the next day, when the children's mother came by to thank us for helping her children," I boasted. I got a huge grin across my face when I told Margaret Ruth and her grandmother about my sister Mary. I continued on with my story, "The mailman came in, and called me Harrison instead of Harry and the children's mother stood to her feet and told me, that's why I recognized you. You are Harrison Obadiah Pike from my childhood."

Margaret Ruth got a puzzled look on her face, and said, "Who is Harrison Obadiah Pike?"

Before I could answer her, Grandmother Spencer became too ill to stay at the table. She got up and excused herself, and asked Margaret Ruth to help her so she could go and lie down.

Marilynn J. Harris

After Margaret Ruth came back to the dining car, she put her hands over her face and said, "Oh, this whole situation about going to see my dying mother has just been too much for her." Margaret Ruth slowly shook her head back and forth and then whispered, "She has been upset ever since we first got the telegram asking us to return." She smudged her eyes with a napkin before quietly saying, "She didn't want to go, but she knew that we must. Grandmother has been so excited about all of our wedding plans. That is all she ever talks about, but when we received news of my mother, she instantly changed. She has been extremely nervous and disheartened. That's why I asked you to travel with us. We didn't want to go alone." Margaret Ruth dabbed her eyes with her napkin again, "I have been really worried about her. She just mopes around the house each day. I am glad we are finally on our way, I just hope she gets better once we get there."

Margaret Ruth was silent for a minute, then she looked into my face and said, "Harry, I have not seen my family since I was an infant, I don't even know these people, and they don't know me." She went on, "My grandmother raised me. She and Grandfather have given me a good life, and I have always been so grateful."

I put my arm around her shoulder to comfort her, there was nothing I could say. Finally, I told her, "I'm just glad I can be here for both you."

We would be pulling into the Oklahoma City train station in two hours, and although Grandma Spencer was awake, she hadn't spoken to anyone. She knew that we were almost there, and I guess she was just too upset about seeing the family again to talk to anyone.

When we arrived at the train station, we were met by a tall, nice looking young man that said he was Margaret Ruth's brother, James. Both James and I helped Grandmother Spencer get up into the wagon, and then we started on our long journey to go and meet the rest of the family. James was very soft spoken and gentle, much like Margaret Ruth.

He told us he was married, and had three children, and they lived only two miles down the road from the original family house. As I listen to him talk, I could tell that Margaret Ruth was right, James knew nothing about her, and she knew nothing of him.

James said, "Mother is very ill, the doctors don't know what is wrong with her, but they feel that she will be gone within the next few weeks, because she is growing so frail." He looked over at Margaret Ruth and continued, "That is why we called you home after all of these years. Mother has always cherished her family." He went on, "Most of us live close by and we see each other often, but we knew that she would want to see you one last time before she dies."

Margaret Ruth said nothing, she just nodded her head up and down slowly as James talked. James was very proud as he talked about his family. He soon stopped talking and we traveled the rest of the way in silence. There was nothing else that could be said.

As we rode up to the family homestead, I was amazed at the contrast between this area and the elegant area in Chicago where Margaret Ruth had been raised. No wonder her grandmother took her away at such a young age.

As we walked into the dismal front room of the house, I noticed it was very dark and gloomy looking. The four of us slowly walked over to a rocking chair where a frail looking woman with soft pale skin sat quietly rocking, rocking, rocking, in her rocking chair. The creaking sound that the chair made each time it went back and forth was the only sound that could be heard in the silent room.

The first person to speak was James. He approached his mother and knelt down on one knee in front of her. He softly said, "Look momma we have company, its Grandma Spencer and Margaret Ruth your youngest daughter, all the way from Chicago, Illinois." The frail woman did not respond or even look at him.

As James spoke Margaret Ruth approached her mother and also got down on her knees so that her mother could see her. "Hello mother,"

Margaret Ruth said as she looked directly into the empty face of the mother that gave her life. Her mother didn't change her expression, she just stared right through her.

Slowly, Grandmother Spencer walked over behind Margaret Ruth and began wailing, "Oh my poor darling, I am so sorry." Grandma Spencer was so distraught that James had to put his arms around her, and walk her away. The mother remained staring straight ahead, never blinking or changing her expression.

Margaret Ruth motioned for me to walk up and stand beside her so that she could introduce her mother to the man she planned to marry. She said, "Mother this is Harrison."

When I approached, I noticed the mother was holding a rag doll wrapped in an old dirty worn-out pink baby blanket. She held it tightly in her lap as she continued to rock back and forth in her rocking chair. I got down on one knee like Margaret Ruth so that her ill mother could see me more clearly. Before I could say a word, the mother turned her head and looked directly into my eyes and gently smiled. Her strange smile caused a chill to run up and down my spine, I did not know what to think of this unexplainable encounter. I looked over at Margaret Ruth, but she did not see her mother look at me because she had buried her head down into her hands.

I instantly got up and we walked outside without discussing her mother's behavior towards me. Within a short time Margaret Ruth and her sisters and brothers, and their families met together to set up tables out in the front yard to prepare for dinner.

Soon, a tall, older gentleman, whom I assumed was the father, arrived and joined his family. He hardly acknowledged his youngest child, and I felt sorry for Margaret Ruth as I watched the father hug and visit with the rest of his children. The entire family conversed and laughed as a normal family, but because she had been raised by her grandmother she was completely out of place. She just stood silently and watched as the rest of her family talked.

Krebs, Oklahoma was a mining town, and almost every family in the community had someone who worked in the mines. Apparently, the father and all of Margaret Ruth's brothers made their living working in the mines. I could tell by observing them that they were kindhearted, happy people. I was sure that most of them had never even been out of this valley before, but they seemed cheerful and content.

Every one of them, except for Margaret Ruth lived within a few miles of each other, and they helped each other daily. It saddened me because she had so much family, yet she never saw or talked to any of them.

They were a nice looking family, and they talked to each other like they were very close. I just stood back and watched as they laughed together, and shared each other's stories.

As I looked over towards Grandma Spencer, she didn't smile at me like she usually did, she just quickly looked down towards her feet. It wasn't until then that I realized they didn't have much to do with her either. Maybe it was because she had taken Margaret Ruth away at such a young age, but I'm sure she was only trying to protect her.

I smiled again trying to tie the three of us together in our own private world, but Grandma Spencer was just too upset about everything, and again she didn't smile back. She quickly turned her head and looked the other way so that I could not see her face. "This entire trip was unusually difficult," I said to myself, "Perhaps we shouldn't have come."

I observed my beautiful fiancé as she tried time and time again to include herself into the conversations with her family, but it didn't work. We had nothing in common with any of these people.

Margaret Ruth dressed very sophisticated, much like a celebrity from Chicago or New York. She was poised and elegant and she looked extremely out of place standing amongst these mining families. All three of us seemed completely over-dressed compared to everyone else. I wore my three piece suit and leather shoes, and Margaret Ruth wore a dark navy two piece suit with a long skirt and a silk white blouse underneath. She wore tall dark heels, with a string of white pearls around her neck and a white pearl earring in each ear. She looked absolutely stunning, but not for Krebs, Oklahoma.

Grandma Spencer looked like the normal wealthy society woman from Chicago. She wore an elegant long silk beige dress with a matching lace jacket and a small beige feathered hat. Of course she carried her matching lace parasol to shade her skin from the sun. We couldn't have looked more eccentric.

The ladies had the tables set up, and everything was almost ready. The neighbors brought in food for everyone to share. It was summer, and the families in the community often ate their meals together. We ate outside under a large tree, because the houses were too small to hold very many people.

With all of the neighbors and their families there must have been over 60 people. They had fixed barbeque pork, a huge pot of black-eyed peas, cornbread, numerous salads, corn-on-the-cob, strawberries, and sweet deserts.

I watched as two of the brothers picked their mother's chair up from inside the house and carried her out into the front yard so that she could be a part of the gathering. James told me, "Momma always loves to have friends over. She really likes parties."

They placed the chair, their mother, and the old rag doll directly in the middle of all the action, as if she were the coordinator of the festivities. The father instantly came over and kissed his loving wife, the mother of his children, and then pulled a chair up next to hers and started feeding her tiny bites of food that one of the girls had prepared for her. I was amazed as Margaret Ruth's mother slowly opened her mouth for each tiny morsel as the father continued to feed her, her dinner.

I was so impressed by the deep love and devotion this family had for each other. They did not see their mother as an invalid who was dying, they saw her as the lady of the house, their beloved mother, someone to be included and respected. I was completely in awe of these people. They had very little, yet they shared a loving unity that I had never witnessed before.

After dinner, the three of us just sat off to one side and watched the other people visit, no one even acknowledged us. I was ready to go back home. We just didn't belong here. No wonder Grandma Spencer had never let Margaret Ruth return before now, we lived in a completely different world than these people did.

I whispered into Margaret Ruth's ear, "I am ready to go home."

She whispered back, "Me too, but we can't get the train until tomorrow. James plans on us staying with his family tonight, and then he will take us to the train first thing in the morning."

It was getting late and people were starting to leave. So, we walked over to Margaret Ruth's mother to say our goodbyes. Grandma Spencer leaned over and kissed her on the cheek, and told her goodbye, and then she stood up and started crying again and walked away. The mother did not respond.

Margaret Ruth knelt down eye to eye with her mother and looked her right in the face and said, "Goodbye Mother," but once again there was no response from the sickly women.

I was almost afraid to tell her goodbye because of the way she reacted towards me before, but to be polite I squatted down and looked into her eyes and said, "You have a wonderful family." Before I could stand up and walk away, her mother reached over and put her hand over my hand and tenderly looked directly into my eyes and again gave me a soft warm smile. When she gazed at me, I was stunned, but I could see what a beautiful, tender person she must have been before she became ill.

It was very frightening, because when she looked at me and smiled it seemed like she had nothing wrong. I instantly jumped up, and wanted to run away, but I stopped myself and quickly turned around and looked back at the frail woman in the chair. She had once again returned to the silence, and like before, she continued to stare straight ahead, out into nothingness.

Margaret Ruth had already walked away, and she didn't see her mother's actions, so I spoke to no one about this. I was shaking inside as I walked towards Margaret Ruth, trying to convince myself that I had imagined the whole eerie situation.

Early the next morning, we caught the train and headed back home. None of us talked much on the train ride back. In my mind I was glad that Margaret Ruth was allowed to say goodbye to her mother, but other than that I felt the trip was totally disheartening.

Grandma Spencer had stopped talking, and the happiness that the three of us normally shared was somehow stifled, and temporarily destroyed after seeing Margaret Ruth's family. My beautiful fiancé sat quietly staring out the window the entire trip to St. Louis, she seemed to be on the verge of tears. None of us felt like eating, so we just had black tea and biscuits.

We arrived in St. Louis around 5:40 in the afternoon, and we quickly said our goodbyes and I got off the train and waited for the train to Memphis while they traveled on to Chicago.

My mind was filled with total confusion. Margaret Ruth's family was a very loving, close family, but there would never be a place in their lives for Margaret Ruth and me. When Grandma Spencer took her away as a child, she severed all chances of her ever being close with her family. She is a stranger to them, and she lives in a completely different world, miles and miles away.

Eleven

Changes ahead

For the next few weeks after my return from Oklahoma, our law office was a bustle of clients. Jonathon had lined up several new clients just since I had been gone to Oklahoma. We took on simple cases as well as very difficult cases. Most of our clients were from referrals. I got the opportunity to help with many modest law questions. I also spent hours reading up on legal facts that I had never had to deal with before, and either way I loved helping all the people. Our law office just grew and grew. We were so busy that both Jonathon and I often worked long hours into the night. We were truly blessed.

Margaret Ruth had written that her grandmother seemed very distant ever since they had returned from Oklahoma. She said, "My beloved grandmother spends many hours each day in her bedroom." Margaret Ruth sadly wrote, "She rarely leaves the house anymore, and she spends most of her days dressed in a house-robe and slippers."

She sadly told me, "I think we'd better put our wedding plans on hold for a while until my grandmother is feeling better. I am so sorry Harry, I know we have put our wedding off several times already. I truly planned to get married as soon as your practice got opened, but I just don't feel like I can leave my grandmother here in Chicago, at this time, and move all the way to Memphis."

She continued, "Apparently, seeing my mother and the rest of the family after all of these years was absolutely overwhelming to her. I don't think she can forgive herself for taking me away from my family when I was a baby. I try to tell her that it is alright, but she doesn't seem to hear me." She went on, "I have tried to cheer her up by talking of our wedding plans, but every time I talk about my moving away she gets upset and gets almost hysterical and will not stop crying. She will no longer even discuss our wedding, so I change the subject."

Although her letter was very disappointing to me, I wrote back and told her, "We will just wait for a while until Grandma Spencer is feeling better."

****

Over the next few months, I visited with my sister Mary and her family on several different occasions. I loved hearing the stories about Aunt Etta and Tyson and the rest of the family after I had left them and I had gone to live in the big white house. Every member in the family still lived within a hundred miles of Memphis. It was comforting just knowing that everyone was alright, and that they had all grown up and were safe. I felt like I finally had brothers and sisters again, and I wasn't all alone.

Mom and Dad and I had dinner with Mary and her family whenever my parents were in Memphis. It was amazing because my parents did not seem the least bit jealous of my brothers and sisters from Aunt Etta's family. They had known her family long before I was even born, because all of the

110

children had been raised on our plantation. My parents always said that they were just grateful for the loving attention that the family gave me in my early days of life; and they were thankful that Nicolas brought me to the plantation, so that I could become their son. I had a secure closeness with my parents that nothing could ever separate, and my parents now considered Aunt Etta's family a part of our family.

Margaret Ruth wrote to me about once a week, but her letters seemed different since we had returned from visiting her family. One of the things that she wrote was," I have never received any notice of the death of my mother." She commented, "It has been months since we left there, so something should have happened by now." She said, "Surely they would have let my grandmother and I know if my mother had passed away."

Her letters started getting shorter and shorter like she had nothing new to say to me. She never talked about planning our wedding anymore, but as far as I knew she still wore her engagement ring that I had given her two years earlier. I went on as if nothing had changed between us, but I knew in my heart that things had been different ever since we went to see her family.

It had been almost a year since our trip to Oklahoma and I had not seen Margaret Ruth or Grandma Spencer again. It had been the longest time that I had stayed away from Chicago since we first met when I was sixteen years old. My grandparents had moved to Florida, so I had no other reason to go to Chicago anymore.

Even all of my cousins were married and lived in different states. Many times since we took that trip to Oklahoma I have wished that I could turn the clock back, and we had never gone. Everything changed after that trip, and I did not know how to change it back.

One afternoon I received a very disturbing letter from Margaret Ruth, she had sent me a newspaper article from three weeks earlier, it read: **Fatal train wreck in Chatsworth, Illinois.** The article told about a terrible train wreck that happened late on the night of August 10th three miles east of

111

Marilynn J. Harris

Chatsworth. The article said that a local train bound for Niagara Falls from Peoria crossed over a wooden trestle that had been weakened earlier by a fire.

The newspaper article stated that it had been very hot and dry in that region and the local authorities feared that a spark from the train engine would cause a brush fire so they performed a controlled burn near the trestle to help keep the dry brush cleared. It is suspected that failure to extinguish the fire resulted in the charring of the bridge.

The train departed Peoria with two steam engines pulling six fully loaded wooden passenger cars, six sleeper cars, and three luggage cars. In total the train carried about 700 people. As the train accelerated down a slope about 40 miles per hour, the first engine crossed the weakened bridge, and the trestle collapsed as the train crossed over it. The second engine crashed into the side of the mountain. Each passenger car telescoped into the next car, and the sleeper car stopped just short of the edge.

The article said that four days after the accident the train authorities gathered the remaining wreckage, and set it on fire. The article stated that because of the accident, trains and trestles would be made out of steel instead of wood from now on.

On a separate piece of paper was a personal letter written to me by Margaret Ruth, it said, "My dearest Harry, I am so sorry to inform you that my grandfather, William H. Spencer was killed in that train accident. Grandmother has been so morose since our trip to Oklahoma that we did not even have a memorial service. The death of Grandfather has just been more than she can handle." She continued, "I am so worried about her, because she spends most her day in bed. A nurse comes in each morning to check on her, and I feed her meals on a tray, and stay in her room and eat my meals with her." She went on, "I rarely leave the house anymore, because I'm afraid to leave her alone."

After reading her letter, I wanted to catch the next train and head to Chicago, but my work load was so heavy I decided to wait a week or so. I

112

could then take a few extra days off and surprise Margaret Ruth and go and see her.

Jonathon had gotten married, and I was ready to settle down too, but now that Margaret Ruth's grandfather had died I knew she would not be able to leave her grandmother anytime soon. I had told my fiancé many times that I wanted to come to Chicago for a few days, and start making wedding plans, so we could buy a house, and start a family. Each time I wrote to her she ask me to wait a little while longer. I had no choice, so I was forced to wait.

The next week got busier and once again I was unable to take off to go to Chicago. I wrote a letter to Margaret Ruth at least twice a week telling her how much I missed her, but she never ask me to come to Chicago anymore, so I continued to stay in Memphis.

One afternoon when the mail came, I received a letter from my cousin Candace, who was still living in New York City. The letter said, "To my dear cousin Harry, I have thought of you and your family so many times in the past few years. My husband John and I have been blessed with two wonderful children, John Jr. and Madelyn Faye. So, now I guess your new name is 'Uncle Harry.' I have performed in many magnificent events, but I must let you know cousin, having my two beautiful children has been the greatest purpose of my life."

She went on, "I enclosed a picture of my two children and myself standing in the front of the New York City Ballet where I have performed so many times in my career." She continued, "I am sure that you and Margaret Ruth are married by now, and I hope that you will also be blessed with many children of your own. Please send my best to your dear Mother and Father." It was signed, "With all my love, your cousin Candace."

I placed the wonderful picture on my desk and I had to smile as I stared at the face of my impeccable cousin. My first love, still so beautiful, now married and standing with her two precious children in front of the familiar building that I had privately visited so many times to watch her perform.

Marilynn J. Harris

"Uncle Harry," I thought to myself. "I think I like my new name." Thinking of Candace made me smile, she warmed my heart; she always did. For a few short moments she made all of the problems of my world go away.

I checked the address on the envelope, and quickly sent her a short letter to thank her for the picture. She would forever hold a special place in my heart, and I would cherish the wonderful picture always.

Twelve

Mine Explosion

Krebs, Oklahoma

One of the first things that I did each morning when I arrived at work was sit down and read the news from around the world. Jonathon and I both felt that our law firm needed to keep informed of the many changes taking place throughout our country and overseas. As I read the morning news, I was shocked by the front page of the national news. The headlines told of a huge mine explosion that killed nearly 100 miners in Krebs, Oklahoma. A cold chill ran up my spine. The newspaper article said that the disaster was the worst mining catastrophe in Oklahoma's history. It was mainly because the emphasis has not been on the safety of the miners, it has been on making money.

Southern Oklahoma was a prime location for mining at the turn of the 19th century. Much of the land belonged to Native Americans, and was

115

exempt from U.S. federal government laws and regulations. Krebs, Oklahoma is a city in Pittsburg County Oklahoma, USA.

The article stated that although the mining company had an uninterested attitude toward safety, it was well known there were more than enough immigrants in the area willing to work in the dangerous conditions at the Krebs Mine. Many of the miners were of Italian or Russian descent.

The Osage Coal Mining Company's number 11 mine was notorious for its poor conditions. This led to a high turnover of workers and the company routinely hired unskilled labor, recording little in the way of tracking to get up to speed. This was true for even the most dangerous jobs, like handling explosives and munitions.

The article stated that early in the evening of January seventh, several hundred workers were mining in number 11 when an unexperienced worker accidently set off a stash of explosives. Approximately, 100 miners were burned or buried in the explosion. Another 150 suffered serious injuries. Nearly every household in Krebs, was affected by the tragedy. Many of the bodies were never found.

As the miners were preparing to leave shaft number 11 shortly after 5 o'clock Friday evening, a terrific explosion occurred spreading death amongst the miners that were at work.

The article read, 100 men were entombed in the mine. It was only possible to get a count by canvassing house to house to see exactly who was missing.

The men involved were the day shift workers. Six men who had already been hoisted in the cage had stepped onto the platform at the side of the shaft, when the cage was blown through the roof of the tower, 50 feet in the air. Flames shot up the shaft to about 100 feet which were followed by other explosions that could be heard for miles. It shook all of the neighboring counties violently.

There were males of every age working in the mine. Some of the boys were as young as nine years old, and many of them were killed or injured. The exact number of victims is not known, because no one knows for sure how many workers were actually in the mine.

Five cages raised men to the surface, and countless other men escaped out through shaft number seven. When everything was over, rescuers were lowered in a basket to search for survivors. Many brothers, fathers and sons died in the mine. The article stated that there were as many as 3 generations involved in the terrible disaster.

I was so shaken after I read the newspaper article that I told Jonathon I had to leave the office and go to Chicago right away and talk to Margaret Ruth and Grandma Spencer. I had no idea how long I would need to be gone. I went home and quickly packed and caught a train within an hour, and headed for Chicago. I wanted to tell Margaret Ruth the news in person. I felt so upset for her because there was a good chance that she may have lost her entire family in the mine disaster, and I wanted to be there for her when she received the news. I knew she rarely followed the world news, so I felt quite sure that she would not have heard the disturbing headlines in advance.

As I sat on the train, I thought to myself, "Oh my poor Margaret Ruth, she had just recently been introduced to her family for the first time, and now they may all be gone." As I sat on the train and thought of how disconnected we felt when we were with her family in Oklahoma, I was overwhelmed by the sadness that we may never get another opportunity to try to unite with all of them. I covered my face with my hands, as I agonized I thought, "Our visit did not go well last time, but our trip to see her ill mother may have been the only opportunity that we will ever get to meet her family."

We would be pulling into Chicago within an hour, and I was anxiously thinking of the exact words for me to say to Margaret Ruth and her grandmother. I was glad to be meeting them face to face to tell them the devastating news.

As we pulled into the modern Chicago train station, I thought back to the first time that I had visited Chicago shortly after the great fire. I was just a child, but the devastation was so mind-boggling that it is not something one ever forgets.

I love the city of Chicago, and I used to come to visit three or four times each year. Yet it has been almost 13 months since I came to see Margaret Ruth and her grandmother, and it feels so good to be back in my mother's beautiful hometown.

As I walked up the street to Grandma Spencer's traditional residence, I realized that everything would be so different now that both my grandparents and cousins had moved away, and Margaret Ruth's grandfather was gone. With Grandmother Spencer's illness, I wasn't sure what might happen when I tell them the news. I dreaded telling them more bad news, but I knew that I had to let them know. The family has already been through a lot in the past year, and this mining accident may just be too much for them. I brought the newspaper article about the Krebs mine disaster with me so that Margaret Ruth and Grandma Spencer could read everything for themselves.

I knocked on the front door, but everything remained quiet. I knocked again, but there was still no answer. I wasn't sure what to do, because in Margaret Ruth's last letter she stated that Grandma Spencer spent most of her days in bed. Yet, no one was coming to the door.

As I turned around to leave, I could see Margaret Ruth and her grandmother slowly walking down the street. When Margaret Ruth saw me, she quickly grabbed the side of her long skirt and hurried towards me. As she reached me, she wrapped her arms around my waist and hugged me then put her face on my shoulder and said, "Oh Harry, what a wonderful surprise. What are you doing here?"

Instantly, I felt half-sick wishing I wasn't there to bring bad news. Before I could answer her, Grandma Spencer walked up and softly whispered, "Hello Harry." Grandma Spencer looked pale and extremely thin. I could tell that she had been very ill.

Margaret Ruth said, "Let's go inside and talk, Grandma really needs to sit down. This is only the third time that she has been out of the house, and she gets really tired."

As we sat down, I rapidly told them about the article about Krebs, Oklahoma. I said, "I am so sorry to have to tell you such horrendous news, but I wanted to come to Chicago and tell you of the disaster in person." I then handed Margaret Ruth the article that I had taken out of the newspaper. I apologized again and said, "Margaret Ruth I am so sorry."

As she read the horrific article, she covered her face with her hands and wept as she said, "Oh Harry, my poor family. I must go to Oklahoma and see if they need help." She stood up and paced back and forth in front of the window as she continued to cry and plan our trip back to Krebs.

By early the next morning, the three of us were once again on the train heading back to the place of my fiancés birth. For almost the entire trip we sat in silence. I feared what we might be faced with once we arrived at the small mining town. I thought to myself, "Margaret Ruth's brother, James was there to greet us last time we were there." I shook my head back and forth to clear away the sadness that I was feeling, as I thought, "He may have been killed in the mining accident, along with all of her other brothers, as well as her father, because they all worked in the mines." I leaned my head back against the train seat and tried to rest, but my head was spinning.

Thirteen

Could Things get Any Worse?

As we pulled into the Oklahoma train station, I looked for a carriage that we could use to take us to the homestead of Margaret Ruth's family. Luckily, we had been there in the last year, and we knew exactly where to go. Of course, Grandma Spencer knew how to get to the property, but she wasn't talking much. She wasn't any help at all. She just set quietly in the back of the carriage and stared out to the side.

When we pulled up to the property, there was no one around. Margaret Ruth and Grandma Spencer stayed in the carriage as I got out and walked up to the front door. I gently knocked on the front door, but there was no sound from inside. I knocked again, but still there was no sign of anyone. I walked back to the carriage to tell the ladies there was no one around.

We decided to go down the road and see if we could find any of the neighbors that knew anything about Margaret Ruth's family. We stopped at the first house on the right. I again walked up and knocked on the door. Just like at her family's home, no one answered.

We traveled down the road to the next house, again there was no one home. I stopped at each house along the way, but found no one. We kept on going trying every single house, but there was no one anywhere.

We decided to head in the direction of the mine, and see if we could find anyone. The closer we got to the roped off section, the noisier it became, and we heard wailing, and crying and people murmuring. It looked like the entire town was all gathered in the same place, and they had been there for days.

It had been six days since I first read the article in the newspaper about this horrific mining accident, but apparently, they were still searching for lost miners, and the men that had been buried alive. The recovery was slow because they were digging everything by hand.

As we approached the disaster area, we saw many women and young children working together trying to find their lost loved ones. It seemed that everyone was helping in the recovery process. It was amazing to see the diligence of these hard-working people. I knew that they had been here since the mine first collapsed, and they would not stop searching until every miner had been accounted for, either alive, dead or unreachable.

No one noticed our approach, they were all focused on the rescue effort. We searched through the crowd looking for anyone that looked familiar, but everyone was dirty and sweaty and it was hard to tell who they were.

Off in the distance, I saw a middle-aged woman that looked a lot like Margaret Ruth's mother, only this woman was walking and helping the other people dig. I thought at first it might have been one of Margaret Ruth's sisters, because they all looked so much alike, but as I approached I could tell that it actually was her mother. Her mother had not died; in fact she was very much alive and well.

Marilynn J. Harris

As I cautiously walked closer to the woman, I also realized the man digging beside her, was Margaret Ruth's father. It was the middle of the afternoon so even though they were covered in soot I could easily distinguish both of them.

As the three of us approached, the mother turned and waved and looked directly at me. She completely ignored Grandma Spencer and Margaret Ruth, she saw only me.

I stared at the mother in amazement, and I was baffled not only because she was looking at me, but also because she was walking and talking. The last time that we were there they told us she was dying, and I saw for myself that she was unable to move or even get out of the chair. Margaret Ruth and I both just gaped at the mother as she waved and then completed the work that she was doing.

I turned to look at Grandma Spencer to see if she had heard Margaret Ruth's mother speaking, but she had dropped down on her knees and she was wailing at the top of her lungs.

Nothing was making sense. I instantly looked towards Margaret Ruth, but I could tell that she was just as confused as I was. Before we could say anything, James approached and put his arms around Margaret Ruth and hugged her tightly as he cried, "I am so glad you have come. Only Father and I and Ruby and Mabel's husbands have survived the horrendous cave in." He mourned, "All of our brothers are dead, along with two of our brothers-in-law."

After he contained himself and stopped for a moment, Margaret Ruth slowly asked, "Is… Mother well now?"

James glanced over towards his parents as he stated, "Oh yes, it is a miracle, shortly after you were here last year, she began to change. She started eating again, and one day when Father got home from work she was up walking around. Within a few days she started talking again and slowly she just returned to the way she used to be." He went on, "She truly surprised the doctors, and they say they will never know exactly what was wrong with her." James went on, "To be honest with you, she is stronger now than I have ever seen her in my lifetime."

James watched his mother for a few minutes before saying, "But with the mine disaster I have been really worried about her." He continued to watch his parents as he talked, "She seems strong, but her children were her life, and I am so fearful that she will revert back to the blankness again." He covered his face with his dirty hands and as he wiped tears from his eyes and said, "I am the only son she has left."

When I looked over at her parents, I realized that they were walking in our direction. Both of them were crying as they walked towards us, but they were trying to smile through their tears. They seemed glad that we were there, but I was almost afraid to see them, because Margaret Ruth's mother had acted so peculiar the last time that we saw her. I just stared at her as she quickly walked directly towards me. I froze in place when she smiled and tenderly reached out and grabbed my hand.

Her mother was slender and petite, like Margaret Ruth, and she was soft spoken and graceful, but she also had the strength and confidence that I admired so highly in my fiancé. She was actually a very beautiful woman, but I was stunned by her appearance because she was no longer frail and distant like she had been when we were here last year. It was like I was seeing a completely different person.

I couldn't think straight, because the mother made me feel so uncomfortable. I asked myself, "What is going on here?" Once again I looked at Grandma Spencer and this time she was sitting on the ground, in a heap hysterically crying her eyes out. I guess she was overcome by the loss of her grandsons. I couldn't understand any of this; people were acting so strange.

I glanced over at Margaret Ruth's father and he looked just as dumbfounded as I did to see his wife completely ignoring their own daughter, and instead holding tightly to my hand. Then of course, Grandma

Spencer was still curled up on the ground wailing. We had come here to comfort this family, yet they were all acting so odd.

I had to stop and take a deep breath. I felt sorry for Margaret Ruth's parents and her brother and sisters for the horrific situation they were forced to deal with, but I was feeling a little bit overwhelmed. When the mother finally let me go, I wanted to grab Margaret Ruth and get as far away from Krebs, Oklahoma, as possible. After all, both the mother and the father completely ignored their daughter, and she is the reason that we came.

As I looked down at Grandma Spencer sitting on the ground sobbing, I thought about running away and just leaving her here too. She acted like she had completely lost her mind as she sat on the ground sobbing in the dirt.

I suddenly caught myself, and I remembered why we had come. This poor family needs us right now, and I must remain calm and try to help in any way possible. I slowly walked over to Grandma Spencer to help her get up off the ground.

As I picked her up from the ground, a woman standing only a few feet away from us began to wail as her husband and her oldest son were pulled out from the debris. Someone shouted that the last of the bodies that could be reached had been retrieved from the shaft, and every one of the people around us began sobbing, moaning and crying out to the Lord. The atmosphere was unreal, I had never seen so much sadness. Every man, woman, and child was in mourning. There was an unbearable sorrow that none of us could escape, and it went to the depth of our souls.

Suddenly a large man, they referred to as Pastor Raymond stood up on a big flat rock and began to pray over the people. His loud, deep baritone voice resonated throughout the crowd. For one moment, every single person in the area of the mine stood still and automatically bowed their heads, and listened to the pastor pray.

I was still in intense thought when I suddenly realized that Margaret Ruth had grabbed my arm and was leading me towards the carriage so that we could take her family to the church building to sign papers. It was afternoon and there was a massive amount of death certificates that needed to be signed. I couldn't believe the ravaging sorrow all around. Margaret Ruth and James alone had lost three brothers in the mine collapse, and two brothers-in-law. The whole situation was just overpowering.

Although I was a lawyer from another state, and a different district, I was asked to witness the death certificates. Because Krebs was such a small community, a coroner from the town of Tahlequah, Oklahoma, was called in to actually sign the death certificates, but they also needed a witness.

A table was set up inside the church so that it could be used as a central meeting location for people to come and get the documents signed that they needed. The event was incredibly disturbing. I don't think there was one family in the community that was not somehow affected by this atrocious disaster.

I saw young women standing with two or three children at their side. They looked pale, hopeless and almost unresponsive. My heart was so torn for these people. I had no idea what they would do now that their husbands and fathers were gone. Most of the families were barely surviving as it was. My heart wanted to help every one of them, but I had no idea how I could do that.

Name after name was read, and the papers were signed. It had to be one of the most grueling days of my entire life. I tried hard to act professional, but I was screaming in agony on the inside for these fractured broken lives. One hopeless person after another walked up to the table to declare their loved ones death. Many of the people could not even speak English, and it was hard to understand the names.

A close friend of Margaret Ruth's parents, Mrs. Harding had fixed a huge pot of black-eyed peas, and a platter of fried okra. James' wife Isabelle, had made three large pans of cornbread and other quick breads so that everyone could have something to eat.

I didn't feel very hungry, but I couldn't even remember the last time that I ate something. Margaret Ruth brought me a steaming bowl of black-eyed peas and some cornbread. So I got up from the table and walked over and sat down beside her and ate. I had to admit, no one made black-eyed peas like the ladies of Krebs.

I closed my eyes for a second and tried to blot out all of the day's overwhelming confusion. I knew that I must go back in a few minutes and finish up the people still waiting in line. All of the wives, mothers, children and grandmothers were waiting to receive their final notice that they would spend the rest of their lives alone. The death certificate was their proof that their loved one was never coming home.

Name after name was called, and each time the coroner called a name someone again started sobbing. Every one of these people were somehow connected either through family, friends or lifelong neighbors.

I was afraid to even look at Margaret Ruth's parents. I could not even comprehend the horrible loss that this family had endured. Although they were not the worst of the losses, because many of the people had lost their husbands and their sons, and they were completely alone.

"Will this day ever end?" I asked myself. When we came to Oklahoma to help out, I had no idea how emotional it would be for me. I know that someone needs to witness all of the death certificates, but I loathe being so closely involved with the survivors. It just breaks my heart. As I looked at the coroner signing papers, he did not appear to be as emotionally involved as I felt. "Maybe it was because I had actually met some of these people before and he probably hadn't," I thought to myself.

We were coming to the close of the death certificates, and it was time for Margaret Ruth's parents to sign the papers for their sons. I automatically closed my eyes and began to pray for strength. I was overcome with nausea.

I honestly did not feel like I could witness these horrendous death documents for them. These people would soon become my in-laws and no matter how strangely they treat Margaret Ruth and me, they are still her family.

I could not bear to look at the family, so I closed my eyes as the coroner read off the name of their oldest son: Benjamin Alfred Pike...born December 22, 1856...died in a mining accident, January 7, 1892....Father: Benjamin Obadiah Pike... Mother: Isabella Ruth Pike...Krebs, Oklahoma.

As my eyes flew open, I could hear Grandma Spencer wailing as she sat at the table next to me. "Oh, please forgive me, I am so sorry, I was only trying to help," she cried out.

My mind was about to explode as I screamed out loud, "Pike!! "Your last name is Pike?" This was the first time that I had heard anyone's last name. I knew that Margaret Ruth's brother's name was James, but no one had ever told me his last name.

I looked over towards Margaret Ruth who also looked confused, and I said, "I thought your name was Margaret Ruth Spencer." I continued to holler, "I was born Harrison Obadiah Pike, and when I was adopted they changed my name to Harrison Andrew Langley."

All of the members of Margaret Ruth's family just stared at me as if I had lost my mind. No one questioned me, they just looked at me as I continued to rant and rave. They had all been concentrating on the names read on the death certificates, until my outrage broke the silence.

Margaret Ruth was on the verge of tears as she said, "Margaret Spencer is the only name that that I have ever known. That is what I have always been told, by Grandma Spencer." Margaret Ruth began to cry hysterically as she wiped her face with her hands, and then glared at her grandmother. "I thought you were my father's mother." Margaret Ruth was genuinely shocked as she shouted, "You are my mother's mother?" My poor fiancé was horrified as she shouted, "You are telling me after all of these years that my real name is Margaret Ruth Pike, I am 23 years old, and I am engaged to MY BROTHER! What have you done to me?"

Grandma Spencer just sat at the table with her face buried in her hands, and said nothing. I could hear people talking all around me, but my mind was a blur. Too many strange things had gone on for one day.

I unresponsively witnessed the last few names on the list before walking away to collect my thoughts. I was literally shaking inside as I covered my face with my hands. I had to think this thing through, so much had taken place and my mind was on overload. Then it dawned on me as I recalled, "She knew, but how…somehow Margaret Ruth's mother knew that I was her son. That is why she has treated me so strangely, but how could she know?"

As I stood over in the corner trying to sort out my thoughts, I could hear Margaret Ruth and her grandmother screaming at each other on the other side of the room. I felt a gentle hand touch my shoulder, and as I turned around I saw Margaret Ruth's mother… my mother, standing before me with tears streaming down her face.

I softy asked her, "How did you know? You have treated me differently from the first time that I met you, so how did you know?"

She looked at me with her gentle loving smile and said, "I recognized you the first time I looked into your eyes, because I saw your father. You looked exactly as he did on the day that I married him." She had tears streaming down her face as she said, "In fact, you look more like your father than any of the other boys." She shook her head back and forth and said, "I never believed you were dead. That is what they had told me, but I never believed them. You had a twin brother, and I saw them bury your brother Henry, so I knew that he had died, but they just took you away, and you never came back. I have prayed for you every day." She smiled her soft warm smile through her tears and said, "So when you said your name was Harrison, I knew the Lord had finally sent you back home."

Suddenly, I realized the neighbor, Mrs. Harding, the lady that had brought in the food for everyone, was also screaming hysterically. She looked at me and through heavy tears she said, "No, no this can't be. I gave you to the black lady, the wet nurse, and you instantly were silent, and I watched you die in her arms."

The neighbor lady then paced back and forth across the room and covered her face, "This can't be happening, you screamed all the way to the black lady's house, and then you stopped screaming and died in her arms as soon as I handed you to her." She shook her head back and forth and pleaded, "This can't be right, you died, and I cried all of the way home because I thought we didn't get you to the wet nurse in time." She kept shouting, "I came back and told everyone that we had gotten there too late." She went on, "I felt like I had let your parents down, because we had gone all that way and you died anyway, just like your twin brother."

I paused and thought for a minute before saying, "That is why no one ever came back to get me, you all thought that I was dead. That explains why I was raised by Aunt Etta's family for so long."

My mother spoke again, "I was so excited to have twin boys, but I almost died delivering the two of you." She said, "After they sent you away Grandma Spencer stayed and took care of all of the other kids for about a month, and when she felt that I was going to be alright she rode the train back to Chicago."

My mother solemnly continued, "When I had Margaret Ruth the next year Grandma Spencer stayed for the first few months, because again I was not doing well." She looked towards the ground before speaking, "I could barely get out of bed, let alone take care of my new baby daughter." She shook her head back and forth and said, "I was so weak and one day Grandma Spencer decided she needed to get back to Chicago. She decided she would just take my new baby home with her for a while, but she never came back." My mother looked over towards Grandma Spencer and said,

"We had never seen Margaret Ruth or Grandma Spencer again until the three of you came here last year."

As I listened to this astonishing story, I was amazed at how the confusing pieces of my life were slowly falling into place. When you learn how the unexplainable lost parts of life fit together to make a whole, it all makes sense. I was not abandoned, like I always believed, they were told that I had died, so they stopped looking for me.

If I hadn't met Margaret Ruth when I was sixteen years old, I would have never been led back to my birth family. But, as I glanced across the room and saw Margaret Ruth sobbing her heart out, I once again felt anger for the torment and deceit that she has been through. What a confusing set of circumstances her life has been. Then the question occurred to me, "Why would Grandma Spencer encourage us to get married, if she had known for all of these years, that we were related?"

I cautiously walked over to Grandma Spencer who was now sitting alone in a dark corner. Grandma Spencer, Margaret Ruth's grandmother…my grandmother; the person who had delivered both of us when we were born. This whole situation is bizarre. I shook my head to clear my thoughts. I then wiped both hands across my face, before angrily questioning, "I don't quite understand why you would encourage us to get married, knowing that we were brother and sister."

Grandma Spencer quickly looked up, pleased that someone had finally talked to her, "Oh Harry, I didn't always know. I thought you were Harry Langley, the son of Andrew and Elizabeth Langley. I didn't even know that you were adopted, I only found out last year.

I always thought that the baby Harrison that I knew had died, because that is what I had been told. I hadn't heard your real name in years, not since I had written it down on a piece of paper for them to give to Aunt Etta, the wet nurse."

I was puzzled as I asked, "How did you find out last year that I was your grandson?"

Grandma Spencer covered her face with her hands before saying, "You told me." I looked at her with a questionable look on my face without saying anything. She covered her face again before saying, "You told me that your first client was a pretty black woman who called you 'Harrison Obadiah Pike' the name from your childhood. A name from the grave that Margaret Ruth would not recognize, but I did.

She told me, "It wasn't until that instant that I realized how much you looked like your father. It is odd, because I always knew you were a very handsome gentleman for my beautiful granddaughter, and you came from a highly respected family, so I always felt you were perfect for each other." She went on, "When I heard your name after all of those years, I knew that you had not died as an infant, and I didn't know what to do."

Grandma Spencer looked over towards Margaret Ruth and continued, "I loved my granddaughter with all of my heart. I took her to Chicago with me to take care of her, to keep her safe until her mother was well enough to raise her, but after her mother got better, I couldn't bear to send her home. The longer I had her with me, the more I knew I could never take her back to live with her family."

She continued staring across the room at Margaret Ruth as she went on, "Her grandfather and I loved having her with us. I thought of her more of a daughter, than as a granddaughter." Grandma Spencer softly smiled as she said, "We enjoyed giving her nice things. Things that she would not get in Krebs, Oklahoma, living with her family. I never legally changed her last name, but we always called her Margaret Ruth Spencer, so that all of our names would be the same."

Grandma Spencer sincerely said to me, "Harrison, I never meant any harm to anyone." She said, "Your real mother, my daughter was my only child. She had many children, and she was not always well enough to take care of all of them. I knew she loved her children, and she wanted to be a good mother, but I watched her grow weaker and weaker with the birth of each child."

She gently smiled again and said, "I only wanted what was best for everyone. It would have broken my husband's heart to send Margaret Ruth away." She closed her eyes as she recalled, "Your mother got married very young and moved to Oklahoma and left us all alone. My husband always told me that raising Margaret Ruth was like getting our own daughter back." She sighed, "We both felt that way."

As I watched Grandmother Spencer, I couldn't help but genuinely feel sorry for her. She sent me away to a wet nurse, the day that I was born…so that I could live. She took Margaret Ruth to Chicago to keep her safe and give her a better life. She encouraged her to marry me because she thought we were perfect for each other. Yet, she bravely came back to Krebs twice, knowing that sooner or later I would find out that we were related and I was born here.

My mind was whirling as I thought to myself, "All of the strange events of the past year were beginning to make sense now. That's why Grandma Spencer got ill and tried so hard to keep us from being together. After she discovered who I was, she tried to discourage us from getting married, by keeping Margaret Ruth in Chicago and postponing our wedding plans."

I looked up and realized that Margaret Ruth's family, my family was all standing in a group and staring across the room at me. My father, my mother, my brother James, my oldest sister Louise, my sister Mary LaVerne, my sister Edna, and my sister Janell were all looking at me as if they had seen a ghost. Of course two of my sisters had just lost their husbands, as well as my brothers Benjamin, Paul and Isaiah. Every one of the men had been killed in the mine. Luckily, all five bodies had been recovered, because it is much harder on the survivors of those who are buried in a cave-in, and cannot be reached.

As I looked at my family staring at me from across the room, I wasn't sure what to do, because everything was so strange and awkward. I had come here for Margaret Ruth and Grandma Spencer, and things turned out completely different than I had planned.

My heart was agonizing for Margaret Ruth who sat across the room looking absolutely destroyed. And of course Grandma Spencer sat all alone over in the corner looking completely out of place. These poor grieving people. Somehow, I needed to help mend this broken family. I am truly an outsider, but I can see how each one of them needs each other, more now than ever before. This family has been through enough heartbreak for one lifetime, and they do not need any additional anguish to add to their devastating sorrow.

It was time for me to face Margaret Ruth and then we can go over to be with the rest of our family. I slowly walked towards Margaret Ruth and she instantly jumped up and wrapped her arms around my waist and cried into my shoulder. I whispered in her ear, "It will be alright, it is time for us to go over and mourn with the rest of our family. We can deal with all of the other confusion later." She slightly nodded her head up and down, and walked beside me with one arm gripped tightly around my waist.

We walked over to Grandma Spencer and had her join in our small gathering. It was time to face our destiny. Our world was not as we had thought, but perhaps finding out the truth about our family will somehow end up being a blessing for all of us.

Although I had met almost all of these people last year, and we were not included then, perhaps things will be different now. Because these people were not only Margaret Ruth's family, but they were also mine. I greeted my sisters for the first time in my life, and my heart was filled with mixed emotions at the lost childhood memories that I would never be a part of. And though I had seen everyone last year, I would never know my brothers or my brothers-in-law.

As I glanced down at Margaret Ruth hiding safely under my right arm, I think I felt more sadness for her, than I did for myself. For today all of her hopes, plans and dreams of having a large church wedding have been destroyed, along with almost everything else that she had ever believed in. Even her last name is not the same as she has always been told.

When we met with the family, each member exchanged unnatural hugs, and then we stood around and told of special events that had taken place in our lives. Of course, they shared stories about the five family members killed in the mine. We all cried together and I talked with each of my nieces and nephews, many of whom were now left without their fathers. Of course I didn't know any of these people, I could barely remember anyone's name.

When it was time to greet my father for the first time, my heart was overcome with emotion. Although I have loved my father that raised me, there has never been a day in my life that I did not wonder who my real father was.

My father placed his weathered hands around my shoulders, and began to sob, "My son, my son, my beloved son. You have come back to us just when we need you the most." Then my father could no longer contain all of his misery, and he began to wail in agony for the loss and confusion that he was grappling with. The past few days had been too much for him, and he could no longer contain his desolation.

We left the church and went to my parent's home. The house was much nicer than I remembered it being from the year before. We sat around and mourned the loss of our brothers and brothers-in-law with our family. We visited until late into the night, and slowly one by one everyone returned to their homes to try to sleep. The three of us remained at the family homestead. Margaret Ruth and Grandma Spencer were talking to each other again, and they stayed in an extra room with two single beds. I was so exhausted, and my brain was on overload, so I fell asleep on the old couch as soon as I put my head down.

I woke up before daylight and stayed quietly in my place. As I lay staring up at the ceiling, the thought occurred to me, this is the house where I was born. Twenty-four years ago, in the middle of the night, I was delivered along with my twin brother, they called Henry.

I have spent my entire life all alone, and yet I began my life as a twin. That was hard for me to comprehend. I wondered how different my life would have been if my brother had lived, and we had been raised together here in Krebs. I would always have a friend and a companion, and I would never have to be by myself. Instead he died at birth, and I was sent to Aunt Etta's house where I would begin my long journey to find my way back home.

As I lay there on the couch thinking of all of the extraordinary events that have taken place throughout my lifetime, I realized there were so many unanswered questions that could never be answered. I was fortunate because many of my childhood uncertainties started to fit together while talking with my family the night before.

Within a few hours, I planned to leave for Tahlequah with the coroner to file all of the death certificates. I would travel with him in his carriage and then I could return tomorrow on the train.

I looked forward to getting away from everyone for the day, and trying to sort out my thoughts. I do not know what my future holds, because in one afternoon my entire life goals have changed. All of my plans with Margaret Ruth for a wedding, a home and a family are no longer meant to be. So, once again I am left alone to start over and survive on my own.

Fourteen

Tahlequah, Oklahoma

The trip to Tahlequah was quiet, and almost restful. The coroner is a man of few words, so we spent most of our journey enjoying the silence. It was wintertime, and we traveled in the coroner's horse-drawn carriage. It was a covered carriage, but it was all that we could do to keep warm against the chilling wind and drifting light snow.

When we arrived on the outskirts of Tahlequah, I was amazed at the contrast between this city, and the humble surroundings of Krebs. There were a large number of farms and newly built homes, compared to the shabby houses and sparse out-buildings that graced the small mining town of Krebs.

Tahlequah was in the early stages of growth, and many businesses were already popping up throughout the city. It was still quite rural compared to Chicago or Memphis, but at least it had a small courthouse, and that was more than Krebs had.

It was late afternoon when we arrived at the courthouse, and as we approached the building I felt a strange chill go up my spine. For one instance I sensed that I had been there before. Everything looked hauntingly familiar, the streets, the old buildings, the run-down houses in that area. The closer we got, the eerier everything became. I was consumed with anxiety. My skin became clammy, and the hair on the back of my neck stood up. The air felt heavy, and I could hardly breathe. My body went rigid, and I was afraid to move. My common sense argued that I have never been to this town before, yet my mind could describe everything about the building in front of me.

As we walked up the steps and through the entrance of the building, my brain could readily detail the massive conference room off to the right behind the thick wooden doors. I stopped abruptly when I saw a large white porcelain statue sitting on a table, right in the center of the entrance hall. I couldn't help but stare at the enormous glistening object. I knew that I had seen it many times before, but that couldn't be.

As we headed for the chamber door, I felt rather queasy because I could recall in vivid detail the description of the room behind the doors. My mind was overcome with disbelief as I remembered the bold flowered carpeting, the maroon antique velvet chairs, and the great oak desk sitting proudly between two vast windows. I could even recall the stale musty smell of cigar smoke as it permeated throughout the entire room after years of being used as a smoking chamber for mayors, judges, and other prominent figures.

As we walked into the room, my mind was gripped with utter chaos and confusion. "How could I have been here before?" I asked myself, "My parents never brought me to Oklahoma. This is only the second time that I have been in this state, and both times I was with Margaret Ruth and Grandma Spencer."

I quickly rubbed my hands together as if I felt chilled from the cold. All of these odd recollections were beginning to wear on my nerves. It was like I had been here before, but in another lifetime.

Marilynn J. Harris

As I stood in the front of the hall literally shaking inside, a black janitor walked by sweeping the floor. I suddenly thought of Aunt Etta and Titus and my brothers and sisters from their family. My thoughts were rapidly racing as I asked the janitor, "Excuse me, but have you lived in Tahlequah very long?"

The man proudly replied, "Oh, yes sir, over 28 years. My folks moved here from Tennessee when I was just two years old." He went on, "Many of the black families in the community moved back to Tennessee when I was about seven years old, but my parents stayed here, so I have lived here ever since."

I was shaking inside by what the man was saying, but I had to ask, "Did you know some people by the name of Etta and Titus Lewis?" I could hardly talk as I continued, "They had seven children, Nicolas, Mary, Richard, Constance, Carolyn, MeriEllen and Ronald."

The man thought a minute, and then he got a huge smile on his face and said, "Yes, yes, Ronald Lewis, he was my childhood friend." His expression changed and looked sad, "But when they left, I never saw any of them again."

I could barely breathe and I was hesitant to ask, but I had to, I said, "Do you remember a little blonde white boy that lived with them?"

The man thought a minute and looked rather puzzled, and then he began to smile as he happily remembered, "Yes, yes, Harrison Obadiah Pike. That's what Ronald told me his name was, that's right Harrison Obadiah Pike. I had never been around a child like that before, so I said his name over and over and over again so that I would never forget it, and look here I didn't forget it after all of these years."

The man acted very proud of himself because he had remembered my name since his childhood, but I felt almost sick and needed to sit down. My head was spinning as I squatted down on a chair next to the wall and thought to myself, "This is where my life began. This is where the neighbors brought me the night that I was born." I put my head in my hands, and I was silent for a few seconds. I took a deep breath and paused and when I looked up I said to the janitor, "I am that young white boy, I am Harrison Obadiah Pike."

The black man beamed as he wrapped his strong arms around my shoulders and hugged me as if he had just met someone famous. He was delighted to meet me, but my mind was in a blur and I could no longer hear him talking.

Although I was just a small child when I lived with Aunt Etta's family, I was starting to recall some of my early memories. I remember coming here to work at night with Titus. I hadn't thought of this place in years. I probably would have never thought of it again if I hadn't had to return here with the coroner to post the death certificates.

Titus often took me places with him to give Aunt Etta a break. I was told by my sister Mary that Titus took me to his work with him almost every night, but I didn't know where his work was until today. No one except the families in the black community ever saw me because Titus brought me here at night and there was no one else around. I had such fond memories of Aunt Etta and her family. That was a happy time in my life. I was lucky that the black community always accepted me, and treated me like I was part of their family.

I asked the janitor his name and I wrote it down on a piece of paper so that I could tell Ronald that I saw his childhood friend. I shook hands with the man and told him, "Thank you for all of your help. So many unanswered questions from my past have been cleared up after talking with you."

The man seemed genuinely delighted to see someone from his childhood. He gave me one last bear hug, and then went on down the hall whistling and pushing his broom.

The death certificates had all been completed so I said goodbye to the coroner. I was done with everything that I needed to do. I had gotten a room at the Main Street Hotel and I would catch the train first thing in the morning and head back to Krebs.

After dinner I felt like walking, so I headed towards the south end of town. Nothing looked familiar but I was sure that this was where my childhood began. It had been twenty-one years since Aunt Etta, Titus and my brothers and sisters and I had taken that long journey back to Tennessee, and so much had happened in that time.

Fifteen

A Day of Change

I remained in Krebs for two more days trying to figure out what to do with the rest of my life. Although many of the pieces from my past had been put back together, all of my plans and goals for the future were now dissolved.

Margaret Ruth and Grandma Spencer decided to remain in Krebs for a while, they wanted to get to know their family again. I hugged everyone goodbye and I despairingly got on the train and headed back to Memphis.

As I sat on the train staring out the window, I realized that this was the first time since I was sixteen years old that my future did not somehow include Margaret Ruth. My mind was filled with overwhelming disillusionment. I felt so odd, because my life had been on hold for so long waiting to get married. Now everything had changed, I had no plans at all.

First, I needed to return to the law office to see Johnathon because I had left him all alone for almost two weeks. Then I must go to the

141

plantation and see Mother and Father. I have so many things I need to talk with them about.

When I arrived in Memphis, I went straight to the office to see Jonathon. I told him all of the things that had gone on since I had left almost two weeks earlier. I also filed all of the paperwork from the Krebs mining disaster. The court house in Tahlequah, Oklahoma, had given me hand written copies to be filed with our office to show that I was the lawyer who witnessed each of the death certificates at the mine. I had been paid in several gold nuggets for witnessing the reports, and I needed to put the bag of gold in the safe.

Jonathon's brother Joseph, was also at the office. Joseph had just finished law school, and he planned to join our law firm. The past year had proven to be overwhelmingly successful for us, and we welcomed a third partner. Our office was one of the first law offices in Memphis, so we were oftentimes overly blessed with new clients.

Having Joseph as a partner would also allow me to take a short break and help get my life back in order. I stayed in Memphis until the weekend discussing business issues with Jonathon and Joseph, finishing up several loose ends. Then I left the office in their hands and headed home to see my parents at the plantation. So many strange things had happened in the past few weeks. I didn't want to tell my parents in a letter, I wanted to tell them face to face. I wrote them that I would be coming home, but I didn't tell them why.

The seriousness of my situation was starting to overwhelm me, and I needed to take some time off to help sort out all of the confusion. The law practice was going well, but I was having a hard time keeping my thoughts straight. I was glad to be going home for a while to talk things over with my parents.

For the first time in my life, I knew who my real parents were and I had found all of my real brothers and sisters. But instead of feeling complete, I felt totally disconnected from everyone. With so many unsettling discoveries, I had never felt more confused in my lifetime, I needed to go and see my parents.

****

After I got home, I sat down with both of my parents to tell them my news. They listened quietly for several hours and just stared at me as I told them of the strange events of the past year. They continually wiped tears from their eyes as I shared the surprising revelations that I had discovered in just the past few weeks.

Many times as I talked, I had to stop and contain myself before continuing on. I often covered my face and wept, because even as I told my story it didn't seem real to me. I hadn't slept well for several days and my mind was on overload. I always dreamed of finding my real family someday, but I assumed it would be a happy time. I never envisioned it ending like this, with the horrendous mine disaster and so much confusion.

Being involved with all of the death certificates was grueling enough, but discovering that I was closely related to several of the dead miners was unimaginable. Then finding out who my mother, my father, and my grandmother were, and of course my precious fiancé, Margaret Ruth was my sister. It was almost too much for me to comprehend. My whole world was spinning out of control.

My parents knew that I had gone to meet Margaret Ruth's family a year ago, but they didn't know anything that went on. I never even shared with them the strain between Margaret Ruth and me after that trip. I got busy with work, and avoided telling them of any of the problems that were going on.

They were not even aware that I had not seen Margaret Ruth and Grandma Spencer for over a year. They knew that we had postponed our wedding plans because Grandma Spencer had not been feeling well. They also knew that Margaret Ruth was afraid to leave her grandmother alone in Chicago and move to Memphis, but none of us could have guessed the real reason for all of the delays. I had never lied to my parents. I knew that things had somehow changed between Margaret Ruth and me since we had gone to Oklahoma, but I kept hoping that our plans were just postponed until Grandma Spencer got better.

Mother and Father looked devastated as they sat silently and listened to my story. My wonderful parents had always treated me with such deep respect. If I hurt, they hurt. I truly was their son. God couldn't have chosen two better people to be my parents. I was so thankful that I had them for support.

Many times throughout my lifetime, my mother and my father were all that I had. I was going through one of the darkest times of my life, and I think I appreciated them more at that time than in any other time of my existence. They truly shared my pain and confusion.

After telling my parents everything that had happened, my mother went to the safe, and got me the piece of paper that my Grandmother Spencer had written the night that I was born. It was just a plain piece of white paper that said my name and my birthdate. My mother had kept it all of these years, ever since Nicolas had given it to her when I first arrived at the plantation. I had never known about the paper before, but I had never needed to read it, until now.

After she placed the paper in my hands, I sat for several minutes just staring at it. So many strange thoughts were floating through my mind. It was difficult for me to comprehend that Margret Ruth's grandmother, the person whom I had been so close to, the person that I had loved and respected for all of these years is actually my grandmother too. It was overwhelming to accept that I had been living near my true family since I was sixteen years old and I never even knew it. The three of us had been so close but now after everything that has happened we can barely even look at each other.

I know in my heart that I was born to be given to my mom and dad. I know that God had saved me from death, so that after living my first few years with Aunt Etta and Titus and their family, I could end up here on the plantation. I truly believe that my parents had prayed for me and God sent me here. I had been given a wonderful life, but now that everything with Margaret Ruth had changed I didn't know what to do. I put my head in my hands and said out loud, "All I ever wanted in life was to grow up, and get married and have a family of my own."

Mother was sobbing as she walked over to me and put her arms around my shoulders and quietly told me, "Harry, I am so sorry. You have been through so much in your lifetime, and you are such a good person. You deserve better than this; you have been such a blessing to your father and me." She wiped the tears from her eyes as she said, "I have always been so grateful to your birth parents for bringing you into this world. I know that you were born just for us."

She bowed her head in her hands and said, "I have always loved Margaret Ruth and Grandma Spencer like family." She shook her head back and forth to try to clear her thoughts, "How could all of this be happening?"

My father sat quietly, over in his chair near the corner of the room, and bowed his head and wept, and prayed silently. He had always been a very wise person, and he thought things through before he spoke. I'm sure he did not know what to say to me, so he just closed his eyes and prayed and didn't comment.

I put my hands over my face, and truthfully said, "All of my life I was curious where I had come from." I shrugged my shoulders and looked down towards the ground before saying, "Finding out has actually been more confusing than wondering who I was." I half grinned, "All of the times I wondered where I had come from, I would never have expected things to turn out like this. I just feel lost. I never thought that in finding my past I would destroy my future."

145

Marilynn J. Harris

As my mother hugged me closer, I know that her heart was just as broken as mine. As she sat on the side of my chair with her arms wrapped tightly around my shoulders, she softly hummed the *Song of the River* to me. I leaned my head up against her head and tried to smile. That song from my childhood always made me feel better. I just wished it could somehow erase the overwhelming sorrow and confusion that I was feeling. I was a grown man, but I felt so helpless, I didn't know whether to cry or to scream.

Sixteen

The Train

I stayed with my parents at the plantation for a couple of weeks trying to think things through. Finally, I decided I would take some time away from everyone, and travel around the United States on the train. When I was young, I wanted to be a train engineer, but since the day I met Margaret Ruth my entire life had been focused on becoming a lawyer, and one day marrying her. We had always planned to settle down in Memphis and buy a house and raise a family. My ambition to be a train engineer had long passed, but my mom and dad felt that traveling throughout the country alone for a while might help me put my life in a better perspective. They agreed that getting away by myself was a good idea.

After saying goodbye to my parents, I went back to Memphis for a couple of days before heading for Chicago. Jonathon and Joseph were working well together, and with their blessings I took off for a new adventure on the Dixie Flyer.

Marilynn J. Harris

The Dixie Flyer was a passenger train that travels from Chicago and St. Louis via Evansville, Nashville and Atlanta and on to Florida. Every day I met someone new on the train. It was amazing, because all I did all day was relax and look out the window. I would visit with someone for a day or two until they reached their destination, and then someone else would get on and I would once again make new friends.

On the third day of my trip, I met a school teacher on her way to California. She told me that by October the United States of America was planning to have the Pledge of Allegiance recited every day, in all public schools. It was something new to the school system, something that had never been done before.

1892 was the year that Ellis Island became the reception center for new immigrants. Several of the immigrants had already been checked and cleared and they were taking the train to their designated areas. Entire families were traveling together on the Dixie Flyer. I could hardly take my eyes off of them, because they appeared so out of place and lost. Their clothes were but rags, and the clothing on their backs was probably all that they owned. I tried to communicate with them, but they were unable to speak English so they remained quietly huddled together always keeping their family members close by. I smiled at them, but they kept their heads down, and even the small children avoided eye contact. They seemed so vulnerable and afraid, and I couldn't help but feel sorry for them.

Throughout my trip, I met grandparents and young couples. I met mothers with small children and businessmen traveling alone. One man that I met was from Germany, and he had been in America visiting friends. While he was in America, a Cholera outbreak occurred in Hamburg, Germany, where he lived and he was not allowed to go back to Germany for a while.

My favorite time on the train was when we traveled through the large cities and I could just sit back quietly and watch everything from the comfort of my secure train seat. By the year 1892 St. Louis, Missouri, was growing so quickly that it would soon become one of the nation's largest cities after New York City, Philadelphia and Chicago. I could see the Eads Bridge out the train window as we sped through the city. The Eads Bridge in St. Louis had been opened in 1874 and it was the first St. Louis Bridge to cross the Mississippi River.

On the second week of my trip, I met three young men who told me they were basketball players. I had never heard of the game of basketball before, so talking with the young men was quite an experience. The three men were tall and thin, and they were on their way from St. Louis to Massachusetts for the very first basketball game.

The game of basketball was invented by Dr. James Naismith and the first game was to be played at the YMCA in Springfield, Massachusetts in January 1892 and that's where they were headed. The young players on the train were three of the original members of an initial team. Having the opportunity to talk with them on the train gave me a personal connection with the game, and for the rest of my life I was always interested in basketball.

I encountered so many interesting people as I traveled, and I learned so much about the world around me. Things that I had never taken time to observe before. I became friends with the all of the conductors, the engineers, the firemen, and the brakemen.

The view from the train window was always perfect, and the rattle of the train racing over the tracks lulled me to sleep each night. When it wasn't busy, I would sit in the dining car for hours, and drink hot tea and eat scones and watch the peaceful countryside as it scurried by outside the large picture windows.

In New Orleans, I boarded the California Limited, a luxury first class all Pullman sleeping car train that traveled from New Orleans all the way to San Francisco via Los Angeles. I could walk from train car to train car, and I felt right at home without ever leaving the train. From the West Coast I traveled from Sacramento, California to Promontory, Utah.

Marilynn J. Harris

A few months after I traveled through California they had a severe earthquake that could be felt all over California as well as most of Nevada. The quake hit in the exact area that I had recently traveled through. I just missed it by a couple of months. The April 19th earthquake near Vacaville, California had an estimated damage of $225,000 to $250,000 leaving one person dead, and numerous people injured.

****

Promontory Summit in Utah, also known as the Golden Spike National Historic site had been chosen as the point where the two railroads would officially meet, and have a big ceremony to drive the last spike to connect the tracks together. It is where the Union Pacific number 119, and the Central Pacific number 60, were pulled up, nose to nose to face each other for the ceremony to complete the track. The two trains were separated by only the width of a single tie. The event was planned for May 8, 1869, but it had to be delayed two days because of bad weather.

There were 8,000 to 10,000 Irish, German, Italian and Chinese immigrant workers that put down the track. It was estimated that over two-thirds of the workers were Chinese. The last 100 miles of the tracks were finalized at an altitude of over 7,000 feet.

Utah became the 45th state of the United States in 1896, four years after I traveled through there. To become a state it was necessary for the Mormon Church to renounce the practice of polygamy, and their political party was then called the People's Party.

After going through Promontory, Utah I headed towards Colorado, Nebraska, Iowa, and on to Chicago with plans to be back home within the week. My parents were right, riding the train was the perfect medicine for me. By the time I returned to Memphis, I was ready to move forward with my life. My travels on the train had taken me beyond my situation, it was time for me to get on with living.

While I was away, my parents were informed that the boll weevil insect had crossed the Rio Grande near Brownsville, Texas to enter the United States from Mexico. Although it destroyed many plantations at that time, our family plantation was not affected by the boll weevil until many years later.

By the time I returned to the office, Jonathon was overloaded with unfinished projects, and he was glad to have me back home. It is surprising how spending a few weeks on a train can put the large mishaps of life back in perspective. I once again realized how blessed I truly was, and I knew that the sun would shine again tomorrow.

Margaret Ruth wrote to me at least once a month, and I in turn wrote back to her. She remained in Krebs and even when Grandma Spencer returned home to Chicago, Margaret Ruth stayed close to her family. She tried to make up for the lost years of her life, and to get to know her brother, sisters and all of 'our' nieces and nephews better.

Through her letters, I also learned things about my past. Margaret Ruth had always been a great letter writer, and I learned a lot from what she wrote to me. We had known each other for so long that she knew just the things that I would want to hear about. Neither James nor my father ever went back in the mines after the disastrous mining accident. They had all lost so much, and Margaret Ruth was there to help them as they tried to farm their small farm and live off of the land.

I often found myself laughing at the clever things she wrote me about our family. I shook my head back and forth as I remembered the first time we went to Krebs. Margaret Ruth was so out of place, she was so proper, and so sophisticated compared to the rest of her family. I can't even imagine her milking the cows, growing corn, and finding chicken eggs.

I thought to myself, "She sounds so cheerful in her letters and I was genuinely happy for her, but I didn't know whether to laugh or cry. Sometimes, I almost envied her, because she was able to stay with the family and try to put all of the pieces from the past back together." Everything had turned out so differently than I imagined, and I continued to have mixed feelings about my birth family. I had a difficult time connecting with my relatives in Krebs, so it was easier for me just to stay in Memphis.

Margaret Ruth held such a unique place in my heart, and she probably always would. Her letters made me smile, and as I read through them I realized she truly was my best friend. We had been there for each other ever since our youth… just like real brothers and sisters.

****

As the years passed, Jonathon and his wife Marie had three children, Louis, Michael and baby Sherry. Joseph had gotten married to Sophia, and they had a little girl by the name of Olga and a boy named Thomas. I was still alone, but I was proud to be 'Uncle Harry' to Jonathon's and Joseph's children.

I often heard from Candace, Diane Elizabeth and Gwyneth and I received pictures of their children. Margaret Ruth sent me several pictures of our nieces and nephews in Oklahoma, and of course I was also 'Uncle Harry" to Titus and Aunt Etta's seventeen grandchildren. I had no children of my own, but I enjoyed being known as Uncle Harry to so many. By the time I was 30 years old, I was Uncle Harry to a total of 44 children.

I tried to live with the attitude that this is the life the Lord had given me, but I oftentimes struggled to be content. I didn't really like being alone. Everyone introduced me to their fine young lady friends of Memphis, and I regularly attended dinner parties with one of those young ladies at my side, but I had never found that someone 'else' to settle down with.

My parents had instilled a deep sense of loyalty in me, and I always thought my life would be with Margaret Ruth. I had a difficult time getting beyond that.

****

On September 8, 1900, Jonathon received a telegram from his parents who lived in Galveston, Texas. They told him of a category 4 hurricane that had ripped through the town not far from where they lived. His parents were safe, but they said that the storm had winds up to 130-150 miles per hour. The weather bureau officials recorded an instant rise in the water level to over 15 feet above sea level.

It was reported that 6,000 to 8,000 people were killed in the disaster. In the rush to clear away the dead, most of the bodies remained unidentified and were buried at sea or burned where they lay. The hurricane went down in history as the worst weather related disaster in the United States for the loss of life.

****

Margaret Ruth married a widower from Krebs several years after she moved there. I was happy that she was able to move on with her life. Her new husband was quite a bit older than she was. Margaret Ruth had helped take care of his wife during her illness. The man was a banker from a nearby town, and he was close to our parent's age.

Going back for her wedding was the first time since the mining disaster that I had returned to Krebs. It was odd seeing her and the family again, I just didn't belong there. I was friendly, and visited with all of my family members, but they remained strangers to me. Margaret Ruth's wedding was the first time that I had seen Grandma Spencer since we had all been there together several years earlier. She too was unfamiliar to me, we had a very difficult time finding anything to talk about.

I could hardly wait to get back to Memphis where I felt that I belonged. I never wanted to return to Oklahoma again; it made me feel too sad. Even after Margaret Ruth got married we wrote to each other several times a year. We had been through a lot together, and though she could never be my wife, she would always be my sister.

I had a lot of friends, and the law practice was doing well, but I had a hard time settling down and re-planning my life. Two or three times I came close to marrying one of the ladies that I courted, but something always changed my plans and things didn't work out.

When I returned from Margaret Ruth's wedding, I decided it was time for me to buy a house in Memphis. I planned to remain there, and although I was alone, I needed to invest in a permanent place to live. I purchased the retired governor's house a few blocks down the street from our law office. I had admired the home for several years. I walked by it every morning on my way to work. It was rather large for just one person, but I had a lady come in and clean it once a week. It gave me a residence to entertain, and it was a comfortable place for my parents to stay when they came into town.

Seventeen

The 1900's

The period from 1900 to 1940 was one of the most important periods in the history of the world, especially in the United States. It was a challenging time to be alive. American's would transition from traveling on horseback to driving an automobile, and watching Haley's Comet. It was the era of Woman's suffrage…World War I…the stock market crash and The Great Depression.

The Great Depression was a severe worldwide economic depression in the western industrialized world. It started soon after the stock market crashed which sent Wall Street into a panic and wiped out millions of investors. Some 13 to 15 million Americans were unemployed and nearly half of the country's banks failed.

Bread lines, soup kitchens and rising numbers of homeless people became more and more common in American cities. Farmers who had already been struggling with their own problems from the drought, could not afford to harvest crops.

People lost confidence in the solvency of the banks and the first run on the banks occurred. Thousands of banks were forced to close their doors.

****

The invention of the telephone actually began in 1844. Alexander Graham Bell is commonly credited as the inventor of the first practical telephone. He was the first to obtain a patent in 1876.

The first long-distance telephone call was made on August 10, 1876. Bell called from his homestead in Brantford, Ontario to his assistant located in Paris, Ontario, ten miles away.

****

Thomas Edison invented the nickel-alkaline storage battery. It proved to be Edison's most difficult project. It took 10 years to develop a practical alkaline battery. By the time Edison introduced his new alkaline battery, the gasoline powered car had improved and the electric vehicles were less common.

****

The drink known as Coca-Cola was developed by a pharmacist by the name of John Stith Pemberton. He began selling his formula (a mixture of syrup and carbonated water) at a soda fountain. He sold the patented mixture for 5 cents a glass.

****

A new type of airship, known as the Zeppelin was also developed around that time. The Zeppelin was named after the German Count Ferdinand von Zeppelin. The first Zeppelin flight LZ-1 flew over Lake Constance near Southern Germany, in July 1900.

****

The first Woolworth's 5 cents store was opened in Utica, New York by Frank Winfield Woolworth. The company pledged to never sell anything for more than a nickel. At first it looked like the store was going to be a big success, but it soon failed and they opened a new store in Pennsylvania. That store flourished, and over the next 50 years the number of stores grew to over 1000.

****

On December 17, 1903, the Wright Brothers, Orville and Wilbur Wright invented the world's first successful airplane. The brothers were inventors and aviation pioneers and are best-known for the controlled air flight test at Kitty Hawk, North Carolina.

The general public did not really begin traveling on scheduled flights until around 1912, but only for short distances. Anything more than about 30 miles was quite rare at that time in history. I flew for the first time when I was fifty years old, but I rarely traveled by plane. I usually traveled by train or ship.

In the early days of commercial air travel the flights seldom operated every day of the week, and the travel was very expensive. It wasn't until the mid-fifties or sixties that commercial flying became popular.

****

France started the Panama Canal project in 1881, but the project was stopped due to engineering problems. They found it to be one of the largest and most difficult projects they had ever encountered. The dense jungle was alive with venomous snakes, insects and spiders, but the worst aspect was the yellow fever, malaria, and other tropical diseases which killed thousands of workers. By 1884 the death rate was over 200 per month. Conditions were downplayed in France to avoid recruitment problems, but the high mortality rate made it difficult to maintain an experienced workforce. The U. S. took over the project in 1904 and opened the canal on August 15, 1914.

Marilynn J. Harris

****

Henry Ford, along with several of his friends, built his first automobile out in an old shed near his house. It wasn't until years later he introduced the Model T. The production of the first Model T was at the plant in Detroit on October 1, 1908. By 1913 he had installed the first moving assembly line for mass production. Most of the cars were painted Japan black because it dried fast.

Over the next nineteen years the Ford Company built 15,000,000 automobiles with the 20-horsepower, 4-cylinder model T engine. It was the first affordable automobile for the common, middle class American.

****

The 1924 Democratic National Convention was held at the Madison Square Garden in New York City from June 24 to July 9, 1924. It was the longest continuous running convention in the United States political history. It was the first National Convention that saw the name of a woman, Lena Springs as a nominee for the office of Vice President.

Eighteen

The Love of My life

One afternoon I received a special letter from my cousin Candace. It had been several years since I had seen her. She told me that she had lost her husband a few years earlier, and she was taking a trip and planned to come through Memphis. We had corresponded through letters off and on, and she knew that I had never married, but I didn't tell her why. Although, we had kept in touch, we hadn't actually seen each other for many years. I knew that both of her children were living in Russia, and since her husband died, she too was all alone.

Candace and her husband had traveled a lot, and she now lived in New York City by herself. She had performed at the Russian Ballet several times in her career, and one of the times that they were in Russia her children remained there with his family to go to school, and Candace returned to the states.

Marilynn J. Harris

Both of her parents have passed away, and she wrote that she had no reason to remain in New York any longer. She told me that she was taking a long vacation, and would be traveling through Memphis by next week. She wrote, "I would love to visit with you and your parents when I come to Memphis. It would be nice to get together and talk about old times."

Even as I read her letter, my heart skipped a beat, because Candace was my first true love. It had been many years, yet I could hardly wait to see her again.

I met her at the train station early one Sunday morning, and as she gracefully stepped off of the train, my heart almost stopped. I recognized her immediately. She hadn't changed at all. My striking 'cousin' was slender, elegant and as attractive as ever. Time had been kind to her. She had perfectly combed dark hair, adorned under a stylish feather hat, and her deep green eyes were still as sparkling and captivating as I remembered from my youth.

My heart melted when she hugged me hello, and then gazed confidently into my face. She gently kissed me on my cheek, and for the first time in my life, I could look directly into her eyes without glancing away. I was once again taken aback by her elegant beauty, and I realized I was still under her spell, even after all of the years.

I actually stopped breathing as we stood on the crowded platform trying to talk to each other; standing only inches apart. I noticed that I stood at least a whole foot taller than she did, even with her strap pump high heeled shoes. When she looked into my eyes, I felt like the rest of the world had somehow disappeared, and the years that had passed, had never happened.

As we stood on the train platform, I finally came to my senses and I realized that the train would soon be leaving. I reached down to pick up her bags to carry them to my Model T Ford automobile. Then we could head to my house in town.

My home was stately, and I was proud to show it off to visitors. As we entered the front sitting room Candace stated, "Oh Harry, what a beautiful home you have. It is so warm and elegant. You have done so well with your life." She said as she looked around the room, and gently smiled a sincere smile at me. "You were always so handsome and brilliant, and I am not at all surprised that your life is such a success. I was quite sure that it would be."

I just stood and stared at her as I listened to the compliments coming from the person that I had adored all of my life. Although we had communicated through letters, I never realized she thought that I was handsome or brilliant. I didn't know she ever thought of me at all. I didn't know what to think. I just stood there staring directly into her eyes, and I felt like a helpless young child again.

Although my law practice had done well, I had an automobile, and a beautiful home, the circumstances of my life made me think differently about myself. My confusing past and living alone kept me very humble.

I naively shook my head up and down, and kind of shrugged my shoulders, I didn't know what to say. Without saying anything at all, I reached over and picked up her bags to show her to the guest room where my parents always stayed. My house was roomy and contemporary, and since I was not married, my mother had helped me decorate it in the latest fashions. It really was an elegant home, for that I was truly blessed.

At dinnertime, we walked to a wonderful new eating house on Main Street, only a few blocks away, called The Arcade. We sat at the eating house for over two hours, just talking and laughing and reminiscing of our youth. Candace was so easy to talk to.

Being with her seemed really natural, we talked as if we had never been apart. We had so much in common. We had both been raised in Christian families, we had traveled a lot, and we had to agree that we regretted growing up alone as only children. We shared stories about our cousins, and trips to Chicago, California and New York. It seemed we could talk about anything.

I had not shared much of my private life in the letters that I had sent to her, so I began telling her the whole complicated story about my family in Krebs, Oklahoma. I told her about the mining disaster, and we talked about Margaret Ruth, Grandma Spencer and all of Aunt Etta's family.

Once I started sharing about my life, the words just began to flow, and I wanted to tell her everything. It felt so good to finally be able to share the pain of my life story with someone, and to let the truthfulness come out. I had always ignored the deep hurt that I felt. I tried to move on, and I never talked to anyone about it. The hurt was just buried, but it was always there.

After we left the eating house, we took a long walk through the park, and then went back to my house for a cup of tea. Candace seemed sincerely interested in what I had to say. She asked me a lot of questions, and she continually added facts about her own life. She admitted her life had not been the fairytale that she had always dreamed it would be. I was impressed by her sincere honesty.

She looked towards the ground and humbly told me, "My husband was quite a few years older than I was, and he had different ideas about marriage. His entire life was the ballet, and he kept our children in the background; the ballet always came first." Candace covered her face with her hands before continuing, "He was a very controlling person, and he was extra hard on me to perform to perfection."

She had tears in her eyes as she told me, "My children were my life, but my husband felt they were interfering with my performance. As soon as they were old enough, he sent them away to go to school in Russia where his family lived." She closed her eyes before going on, "They stayed in Russia, and I rarely see them."

My heart ached for my beautiful cousin. I could tell that her heart had been broken. I just stared at her in disbelief. She was so totally different than the person that I had always put up on a pedestal. Her life had not been perfect like I had always believed. She had been hurt just as I had.

After we had been talking for several hours, she grinned at me and said, "Harry, you are so easy to talk to; can I tell you something that I have never told anyone before?" I nodded my head up and down and she shyly went on, "You know that time your family came to New York for the Brooklynn Bridge dedication, and you all came to watch me perform in Swan Lake?"

I nodded my head up and down again, but said nothing, so she continued, "When I saw you standing out in the front area waiting for me after my performance, I noticed how tall and nice-looking you had become, and I thought that you were growing into the most handsome, poised and proper gentleman that I had ever seen. I couldn't take my eyes off of you, I couldn't believe you were so grown-up, but you never once even noticed me."

I couldn't contain the joy that I was feeling, I started laughing as I admitted, "Notice you, I was so intimidated by your flawlessness, that I couldn't even speak or look you in the face." Once I started talking, I continued on as I looked directly into her eyes, "I thought you were the most beautiful, and the most sophisticated person that I had ever met."

The room became silent for a few seconds, and she instantly looked down towards the table. When she looked up I could see the tears welling in her eyes as she timidly said, "You thought I was flawless?" She looked genuinely surprised. "I thought you didn't even notice me, because you never smiled or even looked at me."

Once again the room became awkwardly quiet. So many years had passed, and obviously neither one of us had ever understood how we had felt towards each other when we were younger. As I listened to her talk about our youth, I was surprised to hear that she had ever noticed me at all, because we were (sort of) cousins, and she was eighteen by that time, and I was barely sixteen. She was so graceful and confident, and she always seemed so mature and grown-up.

As I silently sat there and studied her, I realized that she was being really honest with me. It took me a few minutes, but I finally got up the nerve to tell her everything. I even admitted how I had secretly watched many of her performances, from the darkness of the balcony so many years ago.

I could tell that she was completely taken aback, she had no idea how I had idolized her for all of those years. She looked down towards the table again and without looking up she said, "Things could have been so different for both of us." We both remained silent as we thought of the revelations that we had just shared.

I had never realized how shy, and unsure of herself she was until then. She had no idea how beautiful she was on the inside as well as on the outside. After a few minutes she sat back in her chair, and asked me about Margaret Ruth. I sadly told her, "Margaret Ruth got married a few years after the mining accident occurred, and I went back to Krebs, Oklahoma for her wedding." I told her, "Margaret Ruth and I often write letters to each other, because she will always be my real sister."

Candace questioned, "Margaret Ruth has been gone from your life for many years, why didn't you marry someone else?"

I shook my head back and forth and answered, "I courted many nice ladies, but things never seemed to work out. I was raised to be a very loyal person, and I had a hard time changing plans, and settling down with someone else."

Candace and I talked for many hours that night, and the longer we talked, the more that I recognized that she was just as lonely as I was. As I studied the magnificent love of my youth, sitting across the table from me, I realized how much we needed each other.

When I shared with Candace how heart-broken and confused I had been when I learned the truth about Margaret Ruth and my real family, she got up from the table and walked over to stand in front of me. I stood up, and looked down into her face, and with tears streaming down her cheeks she put her arms around my waist, and rested her head on my chest and we cried together. It was the first time since the confusion with Margaret Ruth and my real family that I truly felt anything.

From that day forward Candace and I were inseparable, and six weeks later I was honored to marry the love of my life.

We had a beautiful church wedding, and we were married by my brother-in-law, Pastor Harvey Jordon, my sister Mary's husband. My mother, Elizabeth Langley was the maid-of-honor, and my father, Andrew Langley was my best man.

The church was packed with clients, friends and all of Aunt Etta and Titus's children and grandchildren. It was the happiest day of my life. Although I had waited a lifetime; my beautiful wife was worth the wait. I would never be blessed with children, but having Candace by my side would be more than enough. For the rest of my life, I would be content to be Uncle Harry to all of my nieces and nephews.

Two days after our wedding, we boarded the train to go on a honeymoon trip throughout the Midwest. We spent fourteen days seeing the United States, and it was the perfect holiday for starting our new life together. Candace enjoyed traveling across the country on the train, almost as much as I did.

****

Throughout our married life, we often entertained in our home; our lives were filled with parties, friends and laughter. We were both Sunday school teachers, and we attended church every Sunday morning, Sunday evening and Wednesday evening. Candace and my sister Mary became best friends, and our families did a lot together.

My wife and I had ridden the train all the way from Miami, Florida to Seattle, Washington. From Seattle, Washington we traveled back across the

United States to Maine, and from Maine we traveled down the Atlantic coast line and back to Florida. We had ridden the train all across America, and most places in between. We had flown on an airplane to Canada, and once to California, but most of the time our adventures were enjoyed through train trips.

We had also traveled by ship on several occasions, visiting other parts of the world. Twice we planned a trip to Russia to see her children, but both times her children had other plans. I never got to meet the two children in the picture that I had proudly displayed on my desk for so many years. They didn't even come for the funeral when their mother passed away.

Being married to the love of my life was just as wonderful as I always dreamed it would be. Candace gave my life a purpose. I had someone to share my time, my dreams and my ambitions with. We talked about everything. I had someone that I belonged to, and that I knew belonged to me. Candace was my refuge, and my haven.

I think I appreciated the gift of marriage more than most people did, because I had waited so long to receive my bride, and I knew what it was like to be alone. My amazing wife was not only beautiful, she was also intelligent, loving and one the kindest people I had ever met.

I realized that being in love with one certain person all of your life, and never getting over that love, no matter how much time or distance separates the two of you, is something very few people understand. It is much deeper than just the physical appearance of the people. It is complete wholeness, and I would forever thank the Lord for the gift of my wife.

Nineteen

The Boarding House

C andace and I were married for many wonderful years, until one terrifying night she passed away in her sleep. The night she went to be with the Lord, I felt like my heart had been ripped away from body. Part of me died with her that night. I wanted to go too, I was ready, but as all widowers before me have learned, sometimes God has other plans.

I moped around my big house for almost a year, trying to cope; but everything was so different with my wife gone. I missed her more than I could ever imagine. We sold the law firm a few years earlier, and my parents were both gone, so my days were now empty and lonely. I walked to town every day and had lunch, but everything seemed like such a waste of time. I felt like I was just surviving.

One of my old clients had offered to buy my house, and as hard as it would be to say goodbye to all of the memories, it was time for me to move out of my large house and move into something smaller. After a year of waiting to join my wife in heaven, I realized I must make other plans. I was lonely, but I was healthy, strong and I needed to be around other people.

Elliana, Mary's youngest daughter had recently built a large house, and she and her husband rented out some of the rooms. My sister Mary was also alone now, so she lived in one of the upstairs rooms and helped take care of Elliana's children.

It was a beautiful new home on a rambling green acreage. The apartments were roomy, yet cozy with lots of closet space. I chose a large cheerful chamber upstairs at the end of the hall. When the door was closed, the room was very quiet, secluded and I had plenty of privacy. Within a couple of months I had everything moved out of my house, and I was comfortably settled in my new living facilities.

Elliana and her husband Benjamin ran a Piggly Wiggly grocery store, and they were gone during the daytime. It worked out well because Mary was there to take care of their small children. Their Piggly Wiggly store was part of an American supermarket chain in the Southwest and Midwestern regions. Their Memphis store was the first true self service grocery store to feature such things as checkout stands, individually priced items and shopping carts.

At the time the supermarket chain was created, other grocery stores did not allow their customers to gather their own goods. Customers would give their list to the clerk, and the clerk would put everything together for them. The Piggly Wiggly stores introduced the idea of allowing customers to go through the stores, and gather all of their items themselves.

Elliana and her husband Benjamin Lee Hayes worked long hours at the store, so having Mary and me living in the house worked out well for all of us. There was always someone there to help with the small children. I enjoyed visiting with my sister Mary every day, and the tiny infants were a joy to my heart.

I was amazed at how successful Elliana had turned out. Both she and her husband Benjamin were very hard workers. Her youngest child was a baby boy named Harrison, they had named him after me. His mother Elliana, was our first client, the very first day we opened our law office in Memphis, Tennessee many years ago. She was the little girl that the store owner had accused of breaking an expensive jar, in his store. Her brother Jerimiah had come into our office to seek help to stop the store owner from hurting his sister. They were our very first clients.

The next day the children's mother came into the office to tell us thank you for helping her children. It had been so many years since I had seen any of Aunt Etta's family, that I did not recognize my sister Mary as an adult. But, when I figured out who she was I was elated to see her again, and we have remained close ever since.

Aunt Etta's entire family had come such a long way since the frightening days of our childhood. My brother Nicolas became the owner of a famous eating house in Nashville, Tennessee. Constance had been a school teacher in Birmingham, Alabama. Carolyn had been married to a senator from Shreveport, Louisiana, and MeriEllen was a nurse in Little Rock, Arkansas. Richard and Ronald had both saved up their money and purchased large portions of land, and became farmers. Of course my sister Mary had four children, and she had been married to my dear friend Pastor Harvey Jordan.

Baby Harrison was only a few months old the day that I moved in. He was the first baby that I had ever been around on a daily basis, and I loved him from the very beginning. Since I had never had a child of my own, helping with Harrison each day was like being a real father. When he wasn't around I truly missed him. I delighted in his giggles, and my heart melted when he smiled, I thought he could do no wrong. I marveled at each new milestone in his life, I knew he was incredibly smart, I thought he was absolutely perfect.

Even as he started to crawl, I was the first person he looked for each morning. He would crawl from room to room if he couldn't find me. He would pat on each door until he found where I was waiting. He was the cutest little guy I had ever seen. As he got older, we grew closer and closer.

I loved that young man as if he were my own. I had never been a real father, so I wasn't positive how a real father felt, but I loved Harrison unconditionally. He put joy back in my life; joy that I thought I would never experience again after Candace died.

I enjoyed teaching him new things. He often sat on my lap so I could read him stories. I was old enough to be his Grandpa, so I had time every day to play games with him, and tell him Bible stories, and teach him to have good manners. Once again the Lord's timing was perfect. Having Harrison around each day was one of the greatest joys of my entire life.

When he started going to school, I was there waiting for him each afternoon. Mary and I made sure that at least one of us was home when the two children got home from school. One evening Mary had a serious accident, and after her accident she spent a lot of time in her room, so I was the one that waited for the children each day.

After the children ate their snacks after school, Caryn would go up to her room to read, and Harrison and I would talk for hours. We could talk about anything. He would tell me about his day at school, and I would tell him stories about my life. We both loved trains, basketball, chess and history.

I had lived with Harrison and his family for almost ten years, all of Harrison's life, and I never planned to leave. But one morning when the children were at school, I received an important telegram from my sister Margaret Ruth in Krebs, Oklahoma. Her health was failing and she was fearful of being alone. She requested that I come immediately. I hadn't seen Margaret Ruth in several years, but I was her only living relative, and she wanted me to come. Throughout the years we had continued to write letters to each other, even though we lived so far apart, and never saw each other.

I packed a large leather carrying case of clothes, a few of my important documents, and of course my grandfather's heirloom pocket watch, and then I left on the afternoon train. I never planned to stay away. I only packed a few essentials. I left everything else in my room, just as it had been for the past ten years.

I intended to stay with my sister Margaret Ruth for a short while, and then return to Harrison. Harrison was the most important thing in my world. I planned to spend the rest of my life watching him grow up. I wouldn't have ever gone to see my sister, if I thought I would never return.

I remember the day that I was preparing to leave. I was upstairs finishing my packing, and my precious 'namesake' came running in the front door. When he discovered I was leaving he got really quiet, he was terribly upset, and he wouldn't even talk to anyone. He just ran up to his room and closed the door.

He was so distraught about me leaving, that I almost changed my mind about going. But Harrison's father had already placed all of my belongings in the car, and he was ready to take me to the train station.

When Harrison came out to hug me goodbye, it just broke my heart. I loved that young man more than anything else in the world. Except for my wife, he was the best gift that God had ever given to me. He was the son that I never had.

Twenty

Back to Krebs, Oklahoma

When I arrived in Krebs, I discovered that my sister was almost bed-ridden. She was thin and frail because she had been ill for a number of years. She had a beautiful home, and as I looked around at her pictures, I was pleased to see that she too had had a good life. Although our past together had been extremely odd, we treated each other like old friends. We talked about our lives, and reminisced about our past.

Within a short time, I became more relaxed and I was glad that I had come. It gave us the time to talk about the things that we had never dealt with. Even in her frailty, she was the same confident Margaret Ruth that I had known from my youth. It was pleasant to be able to spend time discussing things that no one else but the two of us cared about. I guess that is what is so special about reminiscing with real family.

I hadn't had that opportunity very many times in my lifetime, because I was raised by Aunt Etta's family, and then my adoptive parents, and of course I was never completely included in the family from Krebs. So, Margaret Ruth was my only true flesh and blood relative that I could really talk to, and her childhood had been almost as confusing as mine.

Many days passed, and the days turned into weeks, and soon the weeks turned into months, and I remained in Krebs taking care of my sister Margaret Ruth. I often wrote to Elliana, and one time I even wrote to Harrison, but through Elliana's letters I discovered their lives had gone on without me. I was heartbroken, I never planned to stay away from them for this long. By the time my sister Margaret Ruth passed away, I had been gone from Harrison and his family for a long time. I was forced to accept the fact, that I was just an old man that used to live in the upstairs room, at the end of the hall. Harrison would never know the true happiness, and joy that he brought to my life.

I had been writing my life story for many years, and I continued my writing after I arrived back in Krebs. Many of my childhood memories I learned after talking things over with Margret Ruth before she died. Although she was even younger than me, she had learned a lot about our family after she moved back to Krebs to live with our parents. She helped me answer many of the questions of my early years. I planned to finish my memoirs in the next few days, and then send it special delivery to Elliana to be given to Harrison.

I have included my grandfather's expensive gold pocket watch that plays music every hour. It has been handed down from generation to generation, and it is now my turn to pass the heirloom down, in hopes that one day Harrison can pass it down to his next generation.

If it stops working, all you need to do is open the main casing, and place the timepiece in direct sunlight and it will soon begin working once again. I was given the watch by my Chicago Grandfather, Senator Richard W. Bates. It was given to him by his father, he had received it from his father, and his father had inherited it from his father, my great-great-great grandfather Governor John W. Ainsworth. He was the person that the

Marilynn J. Harris

unique pocket watch had been designed for in the first place. I consider Harrison Lee Hayes to be my only heir, because I have no other heirs.

I was born a twin, and I had nine real brothers and sisters that I barely knew. In Aunt Etta's family I also claimed all of her children as my brothers and sisters, but as I was growing up, I was raised alone and my only 'brother' was my horse, River. I had my three cousins, and I had two mothers and two fathers. I had numerous grandparents and I was Uncle Harry to 49 nieces and nephews.

I married my 'cousin' and we had no children, so I leave my fortune to my namesake, Harrison Lee Hayes. Harrison Lee Hayes, the son of Elliana, the grandson of my sister Mary, and the great-grandson of Aunt Etta, the wet nurse that saved my life a few hours after I was born.

The Lord has financially blessed me throughout my lifetime: I made a good living in my law firm, I inherited my family's plantation, I got money from the sale of my house, and as Margaret's Ruth's only living relative, I inherited her massive property, and all of her assets too.

I sold Margaret Ruth's home and with the money that I received from her property I gave a large donation to the town of Krebs, Oklahoma in our family name, the Benjamin Obadiah Pike family. Everything else I had already converted into gold, silver and secured bonds in Memphis. I have those contents locked in a large paid up, safe-deposit box in the First Tennessee bank, in Memphis, Tennessee.

When I was working at my law office in Memphis, I had the opportunity to buy a large private safe, or safe-deposit box that would remain located inside the bank's own safe. The safe was paid for, and it will remain inside the vault of the First Tennessee Bank indefinitely. The bank has been a secure site since it was founded in 1864.

Tomorrow morning I plan to pack my completed autobiography in a large fire-proof metal case, and place it inside a brown box to be used for shipping. The key to the safe-deposit box will be in a small envelope, at the bottom of the metal chest that holds my life story.

At the time of this writing, Harrison is still just a young man. I secured everything in my private safe-deposit box, with the possibility that Harrison might not open the box until he is an adult.

As I sit here and finish up writing my story, I see the irony in the facts of my life. I have traveled full-circle all around this beautiful country. I have met so many wonderful people, and I have been blessed more than one person could ever expect to be blessed. I started out as a twin born in a run-down shack, with beds made out of sacks that were filled with straw, and placed around the floor for everyone to sleep on.

When I was born, I was taken to a wet nurse to be kept alive. In the first few years of my life, I was raised in the black community. By three years old, I was adopted by parents who adored me. I was educated, I had a successful law practice, I owned a beautiful home, and I was blessed to marry my true love. I have traveled and lived my life to the fullest, and yet, I am now back in Krebs, Oklahoma, the place of my birth.

Each morning, I wake up and I walk to the park bench across the street. For several hours each day, I sit and watch the world go by. I talk to no one. Like so many people my age, I am invisible. It reminds me of when I was younger and I traveled on the train. I observed the people out the train window, but they could not see me.

The newspaper said that in August an atomic bomb was dropped in Hiroshima, Japan. A few weeks ago the end of World War II was declared. There are so many changes taking place in the world where I was born. Yet, as I sit on my park bench each day, I realize it is no longer my world. I am but an old man, on the outside looking in.

Krebs, Oklahoma, the bizarre location of my birthplace, and the surreal location that will soon be the place of my death. Even with 71 relatives that have passed through my lifetime, I am once again all alone as I prepare to meet my Heavenly Father.

My body is growing weak and my energy is quickly passing. It will soon be time to meet my beloved wife, and the rest of my family at the river, and I can once again hear my mother sing: *Shall we gather at the River, where bright angel feet have trod, with the crystal tide forever, flowing from the throne of God...*

Today I plan to mail my special delivery package to the home of Elliana. The box is a little too heavy for me to carry, so I asked the young man next-door if he could help me mail it. He will drive me in his vehicle.

I will have the package insured, and I plan to pay an extra fee to guarantee that it will arrive safely, and in a timely manner. The gifts alone in the bottom of the metal chest are valued at around $30,000.

I have also enclosed a personal letter in the bottom of the container that I had written a few months before I moved back to Oklahoma. At the time I wrote the letter, I never intended to move away from Memphis. I was just getting all of my affairs in order to ensure that Harrison would not have any difficulty claiming all of his inheritance. I had the letter witnessed by the Vice President of the bank in Memphis to ensure that everything was legal. The letter was amongst a handful of my personal papers that I brought with me when I came to Oklahoma to help my sister.

January 5, 1939

To whom it may concern:

I, Harrison Andrew Obadiah Pike-Langley bequeath everything that I own to my namesake, Harrison Lee Hayes. I have left him the key to my safe-deposit box, and he has my authorization to open my safe at the First Tennessee Bank Memphis, 4372 West State Street, Memphis, Tennessee. At the time of my death, everything in the vault belongs to him.

Sincerely,

Harrison Andrew Obadiah Pike-Langley

Attorney at law

Memphis, Tennessee

Witnessed by: *Walter H. Pruitt*

Vice President of the First Tennessee Bank of Memphis

4372 West State Street, Memphis, Tennessee.

January 5, 1939

Marilynn J. Harris

Forgotten
for
Fifty Years

Marilynn J. Harris

Twenty-One

Harrison Lee Hayes

He called me his son, his heir

I was uncontrollably sobbing as I finished reading the remarkable life story of my Uncle Harry. I had been reading his life's memoirs for the past two days, stopping only to eat, to use the restroom, and then get a few hours of sleep. I couldn't comprehend that he had actually sent everything to me over fifty years ago. It was like receiving a gift from the grave. I felt sick.

Even though I was a grown man, I could not contain myself. I kept weeping and wailing as I absorbed everything that I had just read. I have never felt so loved, and adored in my entire life. I buried my face in my hands as I shouted. "He never planned to leave; I was important to him." I put my hands over my face, "He called me his son, his heir." I cried out, "He really was my best friend."

I stopped for a second when the weight of his writings soaked into my brain. I said out loud, "Wait a minute what did he say in his letter, he had left me his grandfather's valuable watch, and a key to a safety-deposit box. He said the gifts alone, in the bottom of the chest were worth over $30,000 the year that he mailed them.

I was violently trembling as I tried to comprehend the magnitude of what I had discovered." I shook my head back and forth to try to clear my head. Then I quickly dug through the papers in the bottom of the chest and there in a neatly wrapped box was the 250 year-old antique watch.

It was a solid gold pocket watch, with little diamonds scattered throughout the outside casing. I had seen it before. Uncle Harry had shown it to me one time when he lived in the apartment upstairs. The pocket watch was unique and one-of-a-kind, it had been made specifically for Uncle Harry's great-great-great grandfather, and it had been handed down from generation to generation… and now it had been given to me.

I was overwhelmed. I said to myself, "Who could even guess how valuable this antique watch might be today." I sighed, "And it has been buried at the bottom of this box, in the back of my parent's attic for over fifty years."

I wailed in uncontrollable agony, "Oh, Uncle Harry, I am so sorry," I cried as I again covered my face with my hands and said to myself, "This whole situation is so unreal." I moved a few more papers around in the metal case, and there in the bottom of the chest, was a small envelope with the safe-deposit key. Just as Uncle Harry had said it would be.

As I held the expensive watch and the safe-deposit key in my hand, I saw a small shabby brown bag lying over in the corner of the metal chest. As I picked up the small tattered bag I noticed there was a note folded up inside the brown worn out burlap-type bag. The hand written note was old and faded, but it was still legible. It said: These are the gold nuggets that were presented to me for my work as the witness for the death certificates of the Krebs, Oklahoma, mining disaster, January, 7, 1892.

I was flabbergasted because Uncle Harry had been given the gold nuggets over one hundred years ago. I leaned back in the old rocking chair that I had been sitting in and closed my eyes. I was stunned. I had such confused emotions, I was so saddened that Uncle Harry had died all alone when I could have been there for him. He was such a caring, intelligent person, and I idolized him completely.

I don't want to, but I can't help but be upset with my parents because they had neglected the container for so many years. They cast it aside because it wasn't important to them. They knew how much Uncle Harry meant to me, but once he was gone they never mentioned his name again. I never even knew when he died.

I rubbed my face to clear my head and I realized I needed to go and call my wife, Martha. I had talked with her yesterday and she knew I was going through Uncle Harry's writings, but she isn't going to believe everything that I have found.

I paused for a minute before going downstairs. First, I need to stop and pray, because I don't want to be angry when I see my parents. I prayed, "Oh dear Heavenly Father I am feeling both irritated, and totally confused, but I am rejoicing after reading the life story of my dear friend. Uncle Harry was such blessing in my life. Please fill me with forgiveness, and help me to accept that finding this metal container at this time in my life, is all in your perfect timing. Amen."

****

When I walked downstairs, my mom had a piece of fresh warm apple pie waiting for me. She smiled and said, "How is your reading coming along?" Then as she dished up the warm piece of pie she asked me, "Do you want a scoop of ice cream with your warm pie?"

I slowly nodded yes and I had to chuckle, because warm apple pie has always been my favorite. My mom makes apple pie just like my Grandma Mary did. I thought to myself, "The Lord sure has a staggering way of calming a person down if they stop and pray about it first."

I didn't want to tell my parents about the things that I had discovered in the fifty year old metal box from Uncle Harry. I didn't want them to feel bad, and besides the box was meant for me. So, I called Martha and talked with her on the phone for two hours.

When I talked with my amazing wife, she was excited, yet calm and encouraging, just like she always was. I told her of some of the extraordinary things that had been written in Uncle Harry's memoirs. I tried to hold back the strong emotions that I was feeling, but the past couple of weeks had been very tiring and stressful for me. I couldn't help but rub the tears from my eyes as I talked to my wife.

I told her about the watch and the bag of gold nuggets, but I decided to wait to find out if the safe-deposit box was even still around after fifty years. Martha listened to me carefully, and then she calmly said, "Well, you get everything settled at your parent's property before you come home, and I will get everything organized here at the house." She continued, "You come home next Friday, as planned, and I will have the motor home ready so we can take off on Monday morning. I think we better take a trip to Krebs, Oklahoma, and pay our last respects to 'our' beloved Uncle Harry."

I closed my eyes for a few seconds, and shook my head back and forth. My wife was so insightful, she always knew exactly what needed to be done. She had never even known Uncle Harry except through me, yet she claimed him as her uncle too.

I had met my wife right here in Memphis, Tennessee when we were seniors in high school. We had dated through college, and were married two months after college graduation. All three of our children were born in Tennessee, and we moved them to Idaho when they were really young children. Although they have returned to Memphis for several family get-to-gathers, Idaho is their home.

Our three children are now married, and have children of their own. We are blessed because all of our children and grandchildren live in the Boise Valley area.

In the next two days, I had finished up sorting the rest of the attic boxes. I found many other things that were true family heirlooms. In one box I found Uncle Harry's old photo album that he had treasured so highly. I also recognized a few of the old pieces of furniture that had been in his upstairs room at the time that he moved out. I even found a box of his old clothes that my mom had just packed up and stored away.

The next day I found my old model train set, and then my chess set. These were two items that I needed to ship home, along with the photo albums and a couple of the other things that I had come across from my childhood.

My job would soon be completed, and I could be done and head back to Idaho. Thursday afternoon I borrowed my mom's car to go to the First Tennessee bank of Memphis to see if there was anything still in the large safe-deposit box that Uncle Harry had written about fifty years earlier.

I showed the teller at the bank the paper with Uncle Harry's signature and the date on it. Then, I showed him the key to the safe-deposit box and told him, "I know it has been a number of years since my Uncle Harry had last used the safe-deposit box." I looked down at the floor before going on, "You see Uncle Harry actually sent the key to me over fifty years ago, but it wasn't until recently when I was sorting through some old boxes that I discovered the key and the letter. I was never aware of any of this until now."

The bank teller smiled at me, and nodded his head up and down, and then asked me for two forms of I.D to prove that I was the person written about in the letter. He then excused himself and went somewhere upstairs.

He was gone for several minutes, and when he returned he had an older distinguished looking gentlemen with him. The older man was wearing a neatly tailored dark navy suit, a crisp white shirt, gold cuff links and a fashionably-styled dark tie.

The illustrious looking gentleman graciously held out his hand and introduced himself and said, "Good afternoon Mr. Hayes, my name is Mr. Pruitt and I am the president of this bank." The older gentleman was smiling as he stated, "I will be retiring in a few months, but I am so glad that I am still here to meet you after all of these years."

I was confused as I listened to the strange words coming from the mouth of this prominent older gentlemen. I nodded my head up and down and said, "Thank you, but I don't quite understand. Why would you be waiting to meet me?"

Mr. Pruitt smiled and said, "Because I knew your Uncle Harry. He was our family lawyer as I was growing up." The older man chuckled, "When I was a young man, and I had just started working at the bank, I sold your Uncle Harry the safe-deposit vault." He continued, "Several years later, when I was then the Vice President of this bank I witnessed this letter for him." He chuckled, "I am the Walter H. Pruitt on the bottom of this fifty year old letter that you have just given to us."

Mr. Pruitt continued, "I often wondered what happened to your uncle. I never received word of his death, and I knew that no one had ever come forward to open the vault." He then laughed out loud, "So, you see, this is an extraordinary day for me, because I have been waiting half a century for someone to claim your uncle's fortune."

I was astounded. I just sat across the desk from Mr. Pruitt for several seconds and stared in awe, as I tried to absorb everything that I had been told. I must have looked like I was in shock because Mr. Pruitt broke my silence when he smiled and said, "Are you ready to go and open the vault?"

I was extremely light-headed from the lack of sleep, and from all of the strange happenings of the past few days. I finally came to my senses and answered, "Oh yes, yes, I'm ready." But my body wouldn't move, I still sat there in the chair, and looked confused.

Mr. Pruitt requested two armed guards to go with us to the vault. After the guards arrived, I lifted myself up out of the chair, by pushing off from the chair arms. I felt dizzy when I stood up, but I was ready to follow the bank President, and the guards, to the secured vault to see what had been saved for me all of these years. Uncle Harry had already given me his antique watch, and the bag of gold nuggets what else could he possibly have?

We first entered the main vault door. It was locked and Mr. Pruitt unlocked it, and then securely closed it tight after we walked through. We then walked down a tunnel-type of hallway, and then off to the left where we entered a separate vault with approximately 1,000 small safe-deposit boxes lining both sides of the walls.

Mr. Pruitt politely asked me for the key that I had received from Uncle Harry, and along with the bank key he opened box number 483, one of the older boxes in the vault. Inside that safe-deposit box he retrieved a large, sealed gold colored envelope. He did not open it, he just put it under his arm and directed us down another hallway.

As we walked down the hallway, Mr. Pruitt told me, "The small safe-deposit boxes were included with each vault. When someone bought the large private secured vaults, the bank just included the small boxes with their purchase."

We finally came to another area of the bank where the private paid-up vaults were located. I noticed five private vaults in all, and Uncle Harry's safe was vault number two. Once again Mr. Pruitt used my key, along with the bank key, to unlock the heavy thick door that led to the private vault that belonged to Uncle Harry. As I watched the bank president open the large door, I felt almost queasy. "What could possibly be in the safe, that merited all of these safety measures," I asked myself.

When the door was opened, Mr. Pruitt turned on a single light switch inside the vault, I gasped and I almost hyper-ventilated. The vault was about five feet square, and six feet tall. It was neatly organized, with stacks of gold bricks, trays of silver and one drawer of old envelopes, probably the secured bonds.

Mr. Pruitt and the guards stood outside at the entrance of the open door as I inspected the vault alone.

There were numerous cases full of miscellaneous jewelry. One case appeared to have antique necklaces made with rubies, emeralds and pearls. Inside the case was a paper that listed each piece of jewelry in the case. The paper described every item, and who the piece of jewelry had belonged to. A second tray held several sets of wedding rings, and expensive looking bracelets. "This must have been the jewelry that Uncle Harry had inherited from all of his relatives," I thought to myself.

One large case held antique china, and expensive silver goblets, and several complete silver tea services. That case also held at least five full trays with complete sets of silverware.

In one corner of the vault, there were various giant antique portraits, wrapped in paper and leaned up against the wall. As I glanced through the portraits, I could tell that many of them were several hundred years old. Next to the portraits were full cases of family pictures neatly organized and labeled.

I also discovered a large box containing a stack of beautifully preserved antique photos of Yellowstone National Park. I had seen the photographs once before, when I was really young.

They were some of the original photos that Uncle Harry's Grandfather had given to him on his fifth birthday in 1872.

The park had only been in existence for about six months and it was not even opened to the public yet. Uncle Harry had seen rustic pictures in the newspaper and he was intrigued with all of the green pools, the grassy meadows and the geysers of billowing steam. His grandfather had purchased the professional photographs as a special surprise, because Harry was his only grandson, and he would have given him anything, whatever the cost.

I sat for a second and just stared at the wonderful pictures. The pictures were extraordinary, not only because they were so rare, but because I knew how much they had meant to Uncle Harry. He cherished the unique photographs.

As I stared into the opened vault, I couldn't even begin to guess the worth of all of the items in front of me. It was like discovering a vast pirate's treasure. No wonder it was hidden behind so many heavy doors. Apparently Mr. Pruitt had some idea as to what was in the vault. That is why he brought two security guards along.

When I looked beyond all of the gold and the cases of jewelry, I noticed a white envelope that had been placed on top of one of the cases of jewelry, and the letter was addressed to me. It was in a white sealed envelope with my name neatly printed across the top. Apparently the letter had been placed there in the year 1939, and it had just been patiently waiting, waiting for me to come and find it.

I took the letter over near the light and opened it. The handwritten letter said:

December 25, 1938

To My Dearest Harrison,

Today is Christmas morning, 1938, and my heart is so full of joy, I feel like it might burst. I truly believe that this was the best Christmas that I have ever had. Watching you and your sister, Caryn open your Christmas gifts gave me a happiness like I have never known before.

Since I was a young child, all that I ever wanted was to be married, and have a family of my own. The Lord had blessed me with my beautiful wife Candace, but I was never granted the fulfilment of having a son. I have lived in your home since you were first born, and I have watched you grow. I helped teach you to crawl, I helped teach you to walk, and I helped teach you to talk.

I have taught you to read, and I have helped you each day with your school studies. I have stayed up and held you all night when you were sick. I know the things that you like, and I know the things that you don't like. We have talked of the past, and we have talked of your future. I have cheered you when you win, and I have cried with you when you cry.

I have been with you ever day of your life, ever since you were an infant, and I know the remarkable person that you are becoming. Although, you are not my true flesh and blood, I have loved you as if you were my own son. Sharing the excitement this Christmas morning was the closest I have ever been to having real children of my own. Most of my life I have just sat back and observed other families.

This Christmas, because of the love that we both share of trains, I bought you your very own model train set, with several small buildings, bridges and extra track. The first train set was developed by Joshua Lionel Cowen, and I saw one in a store front window while Christmas shopping with my wife, Candace years ago. I remember watching the model train go around and around the track, circling throughout the small mock trees, and the make-believe buildings. As I watched the wonderful train in the store window I once again lamented that I would never have a son of my own, to share my love of trains.

That's what made this Christmas the best Christmas of my life. Helping you and your Father put the tracks together, and watching your face as the electric train rushed around the tracks for the first time, was a dream come true.

Every Father or Grandfather needs a young boy to buy a train set for. My heart was absolutely overflowing when I watched you jump up and down shouting that the model train was the best Christmas gift that you had ever received.

I bought Caryn a beautiful doll at J.C. Penny. It had dark hair and dark skin and eyes that opened and shut. The doll's dress was made of soft green velvet, with a green velvet hat, and purse to match. Watching the excitement on Caryn's face was unforgettable.

I am growing older, and I know that I will one day

come to the end of my life. I have outlived almost every one of my relatives, and it is time for me to get all of my affairs in order. I realized as I watched you delight in playing with your electric train set, that you are the closest to a son, and an heir that I will ever have. So, I plan to go to the bank in the next few weeks, and get all of my financial assets documented.

At this time I feel healthy and strong, and I intend to live the rest of my life here in Memphis, and then one day I will be buried next to my wife Candace. But for now, I must prepare for your future, and get everything in order.

If you are reading this letter, it means my time on earth has ended, and I have joined my wife in heaven. I wanted to write you a personal note and thank you for all of the happiness that you have brought to my life. The Lord has blessed me in many ways throughout my lifetime, but watching you grow on a daily basis was one of the greatest gifts that he has ever given me. To be able to share your childhood with your parents, and help nurture you like a son, was an extraordinary privilege to help complete my life. I couldn't have loved you more, if you were my own child.

I can never praise my Lord enough for answering every detail of my prayers. Harrison Lee Hays, you were that answered prayer...Thank You.

With all of my love,
Uncle Harry

As I sat in the vault trying to comprehend everything that I had discovered in the past few days, I couldn't help but cover my face with my hands and weep. I came to Memphis to help clean out my parent's attic, but within the past two weeks my entire life has been changed.

"I am not really sure what exactly I need to do next," I said to myself as I wiped my eyes and slowly walked out to see Mr. Pruitt and the two guards. I felt totally overwhelmed and confused.

Mr. Pruitt smiled at me as I walked out of the vault and said, "Do you have a financial advisor?"

I rolled my eyes and smiled and said, "Yes, but he is back home in Boise, Idaho."

"That's fine, I will get all of his information and then our bank advisor here in Memphis can contact him," Mr. Pruitt stated. Then he spoke softly to me, "I was here when your uncle had everything secured in the vault. That is why I have waited over fifty years to meet you." He beamed, "This was such an unusual situation. Your uncle, Harrison Langley had actually purchased this vault several years earlier because he needed a large enough safe to store all of the valuable items that he kept inheriting from all of his relatives. Mr. Langley came from a very wealthy family."

Mr. Pruitt smiled, "I spoke with your Uncle Harry in great lengths as we were securing all of his assets. He came into the bank every day for several weeks getting everything in order. He was so meticulous, he had everything organized down to the smallest details."

Mr. Pruitt shook his head back and forth, "I have never forgotten the deep adoration and love that he had for you. I was so impressed that a prominent white Memphis lawyer, like Harrison Langley, could care so deeply about you and your family, and yet, you were not really even related." Mr. Pruitt told me, "Your relationship with your 'uncle' sincerely touched me. I will never forget my conversations with him. That is why I looked forward to meeting you after all of these years."

Marilynn J. Harris

He continued, "I was so impressed with every decision that your uncle made with his finances. I helped him secure everything in gold, silver and bonds, but of course at that time gold and silver were worth much less than they are today."

Before locking the vault again, Mr. Pruitt opened the gold envelope that he had gotten from the other safe, and handed it to me. Inside the envelope was a list for me to look over to make sure that everything that was listed on the documents was in the vault.

Together we confirmed that each item was accounted for. When we were done checking off everything, we once-again secured the vault doors on the way out. Then we went upstairs to Walter Pruitt's massive private office on the second floor.

He motioned for me to sit down in the leather chair in front of his desk. Apparently while we were inside the vault his secretary had collected several documents for me to sign, and have them notarized. Because of the vast worth of the items in the vault, they needed documentation that I was the sole heir of my uncle's assets, and that I had personally opened the vault myself after fifty years.

It took over an hour to sign all of the legal documents, and give my personal information to Mr. Pruitt and his secretary. When everything was completed they gave me a copy of the three page inventory list, stating every item that I had viewed with Mr. Pruitt while we were in the vault. He also gave me back the key that Uncle Harry had given to me, because the vault, and all of its contents, now belonged to me.

I shook hands with Mr. Pruitt again before getting ready to leave the bank, and then I stopped to ask him one more question. I said, "Do you know where Candace Langley, Uncle Harry's wife was buried?"

Once again Mr. Pruitt shuffled through a few private files and said, "Yes, she is in the Elmwood Garden Cemetery, on Dudley Street." He gave me a small piece of paper with the area and section where she had been buried, and I told him thank you and left.

The directions were so exact that I had very little trouble finding her headstone. It was located in a quiet older section of the cemetery, in a green grassy area surrounded by trees. The headstone was large and very weathered, but it was a beautifully carved grave marker with the scene of a river etched across the top. Beneath the river picture, there was a sentence that read: "We shall gather at the river." It had the name Candace Marie Langley on one side, and Harrison Andrew Obadiah Pike-Langley on the opposite side. Under his name was a blank area with room for Uncle Harry's information.

As I looked at some of the nearby graves, I discovered the names of Uncle Harry's parents and grandparents. This beautiful section of the cemetery had been hand-picked as the final resting place for the Langley family.

Once again, I felt the terrible burden that I had let this treasured man of God die alone in Krebs, Oklahoma. I know that I was just a child when Uncle Harry went away, but I am now an adult and I understand totally the deep abandonment that he must have felt. He was so organized and detailed about each part of his life. He had everything sorted out and documented down to the smallest details, even his headstone was prepared in advance.

I shook my head back and forth to clear my thoughts, then I looked at the gravestone of Candace Langley and apologized, "Oh, Mrs. Langley, I am so sorry. I loved your husband as if he were my own father, and I would have been there for him, if I could. I would have never let him die alone in Oklahoma."

It was time for me to return to the car and head back to my parent's home. Tomorrow I was going back to Idaho. My head was still spinning from all of the revelations that I had received in the past two weeks.

Marilynn J. Harris

Early the next morning, I hugged my parents goodbye and without mentioning a word about the watch, the gold nuggets or the vault at the Memphis bank I returned to Boise to see my wife.

Twenty-Two

A Trip to Oklahoma

It was good to get home. I started to unpack and my wife told me, "You go rest, and I will finish putting your clothes away, and then we'll have dinner." Martha knew that the clothes in my suitcase would be clean, because my mother always washed all of my clothes before I left her house.

Then she said, "You have been on the plane for the past several hours, and I'm sure you are really tired, and from what you have told me on the phone, you have had a very difficult past couple of weeks, both physically and emotionally. You're home now, so relax and go rest for a little while."

I gladly went to my recliner and leaned my head back and instantly fell asleep. I slept for almost two hours. My wife was right, my brain was functioning on overload, and she only knew a small portion of what I had been through.

Martha waited for me to wake up on my own before dishing up dinner. As we ate, we talked about several of the things that had gone on at home

197

while I was in Memphis. One of our friends from church had been in a car accident, and he was still in the hospital. My wife told me that the house on the corner had been put up for sale, then of course we talked about the grandkids and how well they were doing in school.

I waited until after dinner to show Martha the antique watch, the gold nuggets, and the letter dated January 5, 1939 that I had found in the bottom of the chest. Then I began to tell her about the bank vault key, and everything that was inside the vault. She was in shock as I showed her the list of some of the treasures that had been bequeathed to us. We both wept as she read the wonderful letter that Uncle Harry had written to me and left in the vault.

We talked until around 2:00 in the morning. We had so many decisions that we needed to make. My wife and I had always been hard workers. I taught at the college for over thirty years, and Martha was a retired teacher who had taught at Boise High School most of her career. We worked together, and we had planned for our retirement.

We owned a beautiful home off of Hill Road, in Boise. We both loved to travel, but we weren't sure what to do with all of this new-found wealth. This was so different for us, because we had always worked to achieve our goals. We had never been handed anything in our lives.

I knew we needed to somehow include my sister, Caryn, in any plans that we make. She was not as close to Uncle Harry as I was, but she also saw him every day after school.

We knew the first thing we needed to do was take a trip to Krebs, Oklahoma. My wife had everything at home in order, just like she told me she would. She had canceled the mail and the newspaper, and had lined up one of our daughters to water the plants and feed the fish. Martha had also told several of our close neighbors that we would be leaving so that they could keep an eye on our property. She postponed any appointments that we had scheduled over the next few weeks, and the motor home was packed and ready for us to take off on Monday morning.

We had traveled across the country several times in the past few years, so getting everything in order was not something new for my wife. The trip to Krebs was 1,588 miles from Boise. We had gone through Krebs, about ten years earlier when we were traveling across the United States in search of Uncle Harry's past. I remembered from the stories he had told me, that he was born there, but I never knew until recently, that he was also buried there.

It was a long trip. We needed to go through Salt Lake City, Utah, then through Denver, Colorado, and Wichita, Kansas then on into Oklahoma. If we drove approximately 400 miles each day, we could arrive in Krebs in about four days.

Bright and early Monday morning, we locked all of the doors, secured the alarm system, and punched the address to the courthouse in McAlester, Oklahoma, into the GPS, and we were on our way.

It was actually a very beautiful trip. The weather remained good as we traveled through each state. We didn't stop to sight-see like we usually did. We were on a mission, and we were anxious to get to Oklahoma.

We finally arrived in McAlester, Oklahoma, on Friday morning. McAlester is eight miles south of the town of Krebs. My wife had called Oklahoma, and researched some of the death certificate information, before I returned home from Memphis. She discovered that all of the death and burial documents that took place in Krebs, Oklahoma, fifty years ago, were now kept in the court house in McAlester, so we went directly there.

At the McAlester court house, we met with someone from the clerk's office to see if we could find any documentation about Uncle Harry. We asked the man if he had information on a person by the name of Harrison Andrew Obadiah Pike-Langley who died sometime after September 1945. We did not have a definite date when he passed away, only the date the package was sent.

Marilynn J. Harris

The people of the Oklahoma clerk's office were so helpful and nice. They were all very willing to aid us in finding our deceased family member. We knew that the date of the letter inside the chest was January 5, 1939, and we knew that Uncle Harry went back to Krebs, Oklahoma approximately six months later. He told in his memoirs that his sister lived almost three more years after he returned to Krebs, but we had no idea how long Uncle Harry lived after he mailed the package, so we had to guess at the approximate date.

I showed the clerk the letter that I had been sent over fifty years ago stating that I was the chosen sole living heir to my Uncle Harry. I then showed the clerk my two forms of idea to prove that I am the person that the letter had been addressed to.

After digging through stacks of numerous old files, we came across the name Harrison Pike, who had passed away September 23, 1945. After shuffling through the entire file the clerk discovered a second letter pertaining to Uncle Harry's death.

The letter was written by a man named Raymond B. Ewing. Raymond Ewing was the young next-door neighbor who had driven Uncle Harry to mail the package to me. It stated that Raymond Ewing was also the person who had sent for the coroner after Uncle Harry died.

I asked the clerk, "Do you happen to know a person by the name of Raymond Ewing that would have lived in Krebs, Oklahoma in 1945?"

The clerk laughed, "Yes, and he still lives here in McAlester. He is the governor. I'm sure that he is the same Ray Ewing that helped your uncle. The age would be about right."

Without having to ask, the clerk wrote down the governor's address for me. Then he wrote down the road that the old cemetery was on.

It was getting late, so Martha and I decided that we would first go to the governor's house, and see if he was the same Raymond Ewing that was noted in my uncle's files. If he was the right person, I wanted to ask him some questions about my Uncle Harry's death.

The governor's address was in the newer part of the city. It was a large rambling brick home on a beautifully manicured property. We pulled up next to the front of the house and walked up to the front door. After we rang the doorbell, an attractive looking woman a few years older than Martha answered the door to greet us.

I asked her, "Is this the home of Governor Raymond B. Ewing?"

She politely said, "Yes, I'm Mrs. Ewing, won't you please come in? Ray is out on the patio, visiting with one of the neighbors."

I held out my hand and stated, "Thank you, my name is Harrison Hayes and this is my wife, Martha." I went on, "We are here from Boise, Idaho, and we had a few questions we would like to ask Mr. Ewing if he's not too busy."

"Certainly, he is right out here." She said as she pointed me towards the patio, "Would either of you like some iced tea or lemonade?"

Martha answered, "Oh, a glass of lemonade sounds wonderful. Can I help you with anything?"

The ladies both walked into the kitchen as I went out to the patio to meet Mr. Ewing. I held out my hand and introduced myself to both Mr. Ewing and his neighbor, and then we all sat down and I began to explain why we had come to Oklahoma. I stated, "We came to check on the remains of a man by the name of Harrison Pike who died about fifty years ago."

Mr. Ewing thought for a second, and then he jumped up out of his chair and shouted, "Yes, yes Mr. Pike. He was such a wonderful old gentleman." He shook his head back and forth and then sat back down in his chair and said, "That was such a strange situation. I was only nineteen years old, and I had just moved into the apartment house where Mr. Pike lived. The rooms were cheap, and I had rented the room that was right next door to him."

The governor got an odd look on his face as he continued, "He seemed so withdrawn and lonely. I couldn't believe that he didn't have any family around because he was such a nice person and he was so interesting to talk to. I don't think he had any friends either because he told me that he had moved to Oklahoma to take care of his sister, and after she died he was left in town all alone. The only reason that I even knew his last name was Pike was because I saw a paper on his dresser after he had died. It stated that he had donated some money to the town of Krebs, Oklahoma, in his family name, and the last name was Pike. I knew his name was Harrison, so Harrison Pike was what was put on the death certificate. Even the owner of the boarding house knew nothing about him."

Mr. Ewing looked at me and said, "I really think his life was different before he came to Oklahoma to be with his sister. He seemed extremely educated and dignified, and even as an older gentlemen he dressed really well, but he appeared so sad and lonely. I never saw him talk to anyone else, only me, but he was very proper and polite."

He went on, "I had only lived next-door to him for about a month when he asked me if I would help him mail a package to Memphis, Tennessee. The box was too large for him to carry, so I was more than happy to help him out. I had an old farm truck that my dad had given to me, so I drove him in my truck to mail the package. After we returned from mailing the package, I helped him get out of the truck and he went straight to his room, and sat in his chair without saying a word."

Mr. Ewing shook his head back and forth, then ran his hand across his face before continuing on, "We had only been back to the apartment for about thirty minutes when I got a funny feeling, so I went back over to check on him. He had seemed extremely quiet and despondent on our way home after mailing the package. I don't think he talked at all. That is what gave me such a bad feeling about everything."

He said, "When I went back to his room, I knocked, and then went on in. Mr. Ewing had a troubling look on his face as he quietly said, Mr. Hayes, he was dead in his chair, right where I had left him." He rubbed his hands across his face, "I had just taken him home." He looked at me and grimaced, "I barely knew the man's name, and yet, I was the one who called the coroner. I was just nineteen years old, and I had to call the coroner for the death of my next-door neighbor. I had never seen anyone die before. That's why I remember it like it was yesterday."

He went on, "That is the only reason my name was even in his file. He had no one else, and I knew nothing about the man, only that his name was Harrison Pike. I told the coroner's office that he had mailed a package earlier in the day to someone in Memphis, Tennessee, but they could find no record of a Harrison Pike in Memphis. They filed the death certificate under the only name that I had heard, Harrison Pike. I didn't even know the man's middle name, and there was no one we could ask. We knew the exact date that he died, and the coroner knew it was natural causes, so they just buried him at the old cemetery. Out where all of the miners had been buried."

I covered my face with both hands for one second and then I said, "You could not find the name Harrison Pike in Memphis, Tennessee, because his legal adoptive name was Harrison Andrew Langley. He was a prominent lawyer, and his adoptive parents were some of the richest plantation owners in Memphis." I paused and look down towards the ground, and then I pulled out the two letters that I had been given. First the letter stating that I was his 'chosen' sole heir, and then the personal letter that he had written to me.

I told the governor, "I was the person in Memphis, Tennessee that he was mailing the package to, but my mother put the box up in the attic and forgot about it. I just found it last week while I was cleaning out my parent's attic. It had been mailed to me over fifty years ago."

Marilynn J. Harris

Mr. Ewing looked at me and questioned, "He was a prominent Memphis lawyer?" He shook his head back and forth, "You know Mr. Hayes, even at nineteen years old I knew that there was more to his life story than what I could see."

As we talked, Mr. Ewing's wife, Tammy walked out with a tray of lemonade and a plate full of small sandwiches and fresh fruit. All of the people of Oklahoma were so friendly and hospitable. We soon realized that if you were in their home…they always fed you. When we were finished eating, I asked the governor, "Do you know where my Uncle Harry is buried."

"Oh certainly I do, I have visited it a couple of times throughout the years." He again looked sullen as he stated, "I was the only person at his graveside service. I felt like I should be there, since I was the one who found him when he passed away. Would you like me to take you to the cemetery?" He told me, "The old cemetery is about five miles from here. His grave is a little difficult to find, and I haven't been there in a long time, but I am quite sure I can still find it."

The neighbor man said his goodbyes, and Martha and I, and Mr. and Mrs. Ewing got in the governor's Chevy Impala, and headed for the cemetery. We were soon traveling down a long country road. The old dirt road was completely empty; we never passed one other car. Within a half an hour of leaving the governor's house, we came to an old neglected cemetery on the outskirts of the city. The cemetery looked like it had been abandoned years earlier. The four of us got out of the car and walked up the hill towards the back of the grounds.

The entire cemetery appeared run-down and forgotten. It was the complete opposite of the beautiful setting where Uncle Harry's wife was buried back in Memphis. The few gravestones on the hillside were toppled over or broken. Most of the graves had only a small stone slab, buried in the dirt with the person's name engraved across the stone.

Finding the abandoned grave of Uncle Harry amongst the weeds and wildflowers turned out to be a little harder than we first thought it would be. Fifty years is a long time for an old run-down abandoned cemetery. The cemetery had not been utilized in years, and most likely the family members that were alive fifty years ago are now gone.

It was the governor's wife, Tammy who finally discovered the partially buried small slab that had Uncle Harry's name on it. All the simple gravestone said was, Harrison Pike, died September 23, 1945.

Both Martha and I wiped tears from our eyes as I knelt down on my knees to clear the dirt and years of neglect away from the gravestone of my beloved Uncle Harry. Raymond Ewing and his wife, Tammy stood silently behind us rejoicing in the fact that the lonely distinguished gentlemen that Mr. Ewing had buried fifty years ago, was finally going home. Harrison Obadiah Pike would once again be reunited with his family.

*****

With the help of our new friend Governor Ewing, we had Uncle Harry's body exhumed and sent to Memphis, Tennessee, 392 miles away. We planned a proper burial and graveside service for two weeks from Tuesday, on May 17, 1995.

After making all of the arrangements in McAlester, Oklahoma, Martha and I drove on to Memphis to prepare for his funeral. After more than fifty years, we knew that there would be very few people left in Memphis who still remembered my Uncle Harry, so we planned a small graveside service with only close family members.

We put the obituary in the Memphis newspaper, announcing that a graveside service for Harrison Andrew Obadiah Pike-Langley would be held at the Elmwood Garden Cemetery, on Dudley Street, at 2:00 P.M. on Tuesday, May 17th. The article said that my uncle, Harrison Langley had once been a prominent lawyer in Memphis and had passed away over fifty years ago in a small town in Krebs, Oklahoma. The obituary stated that the family had never given Mr. Langley a proper funeral ceremony and they wanted to honor his life by burying his remains next to his beloved wife, Candace Langley.

Martha made arrangements for every one of our children and their spouses to fly in to Memphis to honor the beloved Uncle Harry. Our children had been hearing stories about Uncle Harry all of their lives, so they were anxious to come pay their respects. Five of our seven grandchildren were also coming for the memorial.

We told all of our children the day that we left Boise that we were heading to Oklahoma in search of Uncle Harry's grave. We wanted them to prepare their schedules so that we could fly them in for a funeral service after all of the arrangements were decided.

Several weeks had passed since my sister's back surgery and Caryn was feeling much better. So, Caryn and her husband Eugene were also coming to Memphis to pay their respects to Uncle Harry.

My parent's would be moving within the week, so Martha and I and my sister Caryn felt that this would be a great time for one last family reunion with all of the kids in our parent's backyard. Their house was nearly empty, and the movers would be finished by the beginning of next week, then the house would be vacant. But for now they still have their magnificent backyard for one last gathering after the graveside service. Caryn's daughter and her husband had decided to come too, and they only lived about 480 miles away, so they can easily drive to Memphis.

I planned to speak at the service, and my cousin, Pastor Jeremiah Jordon would read from the Bible and say a prayer. Jeremiah was my mother's brother's son, and he pastored the old church where my grandfather once preached. Jeremiah was only fourteen months younger than me, so we had been raised together here in Memphis, and remained close.

My wife ordered several colorful flower arrangements, for both the cemetery and for the gathering at my parent's house afterwards. We knew that it would be a small service, but we were treating the funeral as if Uncle Harry had just recently died and there would be a lot of people there. Although it still disturbed me that I was not there when he needed me, I hoped that this would help settle some of my confusion. He had meant more to me than words could ever express.

Martha arranged for tables, chairs, and a large tent to be delivered for the Tuesday festivities in my parent's backyard. My wife was an organizer and she could put a large dinner party together in just two or three hours if she needed to. I have watched her organize whole conferences.

She was having the meal catered by a local catering company, and they would do all of the setting up, serving and clean up so that we would be able to visit with our guests. Of course, she had ordered extra food because we had no idea how many neighbors or church friends would come by, but Martha always had enough food prepared to serve an entire army.

Around 1:00 P.M. on Tuesday the day of the service, our family left for the cemetery to attend the long awaited funeral of my wonderful uncle and best friend, Harrison Andrew Obadiah Pike-Langley. Our parents, and my sister Caryn and her family followed in the cars behind.

While we were driving to the cemetery, my mind began to race as I struggled with the various feelings that I had been dealing with in the past month. I thought to myself, "There has been so much to think about both good, bad and confusing. Everything from cleaning out my parent's attic, and sorting through generations of memories, to selling my childhood home and never being able to return there again. Then finding Uncle Harry's memoirs that had been sent fifty years earlier."

My mind kept whirling as I thought, "What would my life have been like if I had been given the metal chest, and all of this information when I was young. It would have definitely changed my life."

I shook my head to try to clear my thoughts, but my mind kept reflecting, "Of course I feel totally blessed to be called my uncle's heir, and now I know that I meant as much to him as he did to me, but inheriting all of his wealth was a total shock. I had no idea that he was even wealthy." My mind was on overload. I felt both joy and regret.

As our funeral party pulled up to the designated section of the cemetery where Uncle Harry's funeral service was to take place, we were surprised to see a large mass of people already congregated near the gravesite area. We feared that there was another funeral going on close by, but as we got out of our vehicles and walked over towards the crowd, I realized that I recognized many people in the group. They were friends, neighbors and acquaintances, and they were there for Uncle Harry's funeral. I nodded my head as I saw childhood friends from school, along with their spouses and older family members. Many of them I had not seen in years.

I was pleased to see Walter H. Pruitt, the President of the First Tennessee Bank of Memphis. He was there along with a lady, whom I presumed to be his wife, and several of the personnel that worked at his bank. I held out my hand and told him, "Thank you for coming."

Next, I saw my new friend Governor Ray Ewing. He instantly gave me a brotherly hug, and as we hugged, he quietly said in my ear, "I wouldn't miss this for the world." I was pleased to have him there, because he was the only person present, at the first funeral for Uncle Harry, and he had helped us so much lately.

I gently put my arms around his sweet wife, Tammy and told her, "Thank you for coming."

I was absolutely stunned as I watched family after family walk up to join our humble celebration. Many of the older people walked with canes or were pushed in wheelchairs. They were the children of people that my Uncle Harry had helped during his years as a lawyer, or as a Sunday school teacher.

I was told by several in the group how Harrison Langley had helped so many of the African-American families in the community. They said that he was a friend to everyone, no matter what their situation or color, and they had come to the graveside service to pay their respects for the help he had given to their families.

I was told that he was always there to help with the smallest circumstances up to the largest legal questions. He helped people get jobs, and he had helped many families keep their homes. After listening to everyone share their stories, I realized that my uncle must have been the lawyer for half of Memphis. I had no idea. He was just my Uncle Harry when I was growing up. He was the person waiting for me each day, when I came home from school. He was the person I talked to, the person I played chess with, the person who called me his heir. I was in awe. It had been over fifty years since Uncle Harry had been around and yet the stories of his benevolence have been passed down from generation to generation.

Many of my parent's friends from their store, and their neighbors were also there to pay their respects. Much to our surprise, our small intimate graveside service kept growing and growing as people came in droves to pay their regards to the family of Harrison Andrew Obadiah Pike-Langley.

I could not stop the tears from running down my face as I realized the magnitude of this joyous celebration. I was celebrating the life of my best friend, Uncle Harry, and in my heart, this was the tribute that I thought my Uncle Harry deserved, but I was amazed to see that so many other people were there to rejoice with me.

Person after person shook my hand and told me that they too had always called Harrison Langley, Uncle Harry. I cannot even guess the total of 'adopted' nieces and nephews that were there to pay their respects that day, but many of them were in there eighties or nineties.

After I spoke, I thanked everyone for coming and invited them to the dinner at my parent's home. Many people had already taken food by the house, so I knew we would have plenty for everyone. Then my cousin Pastor Jeramiah Jordan came forward to pray and conclude the ceremony.

Marilynn J. Harris

Jeramiah had a wonderful deep tenor voice and he reverently led us all in singing my Uncle Harry's favorite hymn; the song of the river. We had the words to the old hymn written on a large sign so that everyone could sing along. It was a perfect ending to a perfect day. My heart overflowed as I closed my eyes and listened to the voices singing all around me. The beautiful sounds softly resonated from tree to tree throughout the cemetery. With my eyes closed the voices sounded like a multitude of angels singing,

"Shall we gather at the river, where bright angel feet have trod, with its crystal tide forever, flowing by the throne of God.

Yes, we'll gather at the river, the beautiful, the beautiful river, gather with the saints at the river that flows by the throne of God.

Soon we'll reach the shining river, soon our pilgrimage will cease, soon our happy hearts will quiver with the melody of peace.

Yes, we'll gather at the river, the beautiful the beautiful river, gather with the saints at the river that flows by the throne of God."

Harrison Obadiah Pike had traveled a long journey throughout his lifetime, but he was finally home; buried next to his cherished wife, Candace. I completed the service as I placed a white rose on the gravestone of my unforgettable Uncle Harry and said, "Rest in peace my beloved friend. I'll meet you at the river."

Amen